THE TRAINING PATIENT

THE TRAINING PATIENT
A Novel

Anna Fodorova

KARNAC

First published in 2015 by
Karnac Books Ltd
118 Finchley Road
London NW3 5HT

British Library Cataloguing in Publication Data

A C.I.P. for this book is available from the British Library

ISBN-13: 978-1-78220-220-2

Typeset by V Publishing Solutions Pvt Ltd., Chennai, India

Printed in Great Britain by TJ International Ltd, Padstow, Cornwall

www.karnacbooks.com

For my daughter

ONE

The call came one Friday morning while Gail was still in bed. "I've got news," Joanna Wilson announced. Joanna was in charge of referrals. "We've been contacted by an Eastern European: from where momentarily escapes me. He's looking for a therapist in your neck of the woods."

Gail sat up. Finally! She had always been sceptical about life-changing moments. But now she caught herself thinking— could this be one of those? Could it be that, despite her "neck of the woods" having presented to Joanna a territory as baffling as the old communist bloc, her fortunes had turned? She pressed the phone to her ear with such eagerness that just as Joanna said, "In case you're not ready—" Gail cut her off.

To complete your psychotherapy qualification you were asked to deliver an in-depth case study. To pen such a study you had to be seeing a training patient. Ideally, this patient or client—those terms were forever disputed—would come to you through your institute. Simple as this might sound it was not. That everyone in her year had already secured such a person caused Gail uncomfortable envy. Everyone but her. Juliet Pinchfield had one, so did Nigel Whale. Karla Urbanova even had two, in case she healed one prematurely. With referrals in short supply Gail didn't take long to notice that a south-of-the

1

river address wasn't exactly a bonus. Ever since Freud found a refuge in the hills above Swiss Cottage, north London had reigned as psycho-land. And somehow it followed that all the needy, the depressed, and the suicidal also resided in these higher, more affluent parts. As if the lowlands around New Cross bred only happiness.

It took an eternity for Joanna to pick up again. "Sorry Gail, I've got the builders in. Otherwise I'd have done a personal assessment. You'll be pleased to hear his English is pretty good, even on the phone." *His* English. For some reason Gail had assumed, hoped in fact for the Eastern European to be a woman. "An articulate chap. Projects a great deal. Went on and on about his wife, her and her terror ..." Here Joanna paused and for an instant Gail panicked—had she disconnected them again? Then she understood—Joanna was merely practising with her how to cope with *not knowing. Not knowing* the nature of the Eastern European's wife's terror and with it all the innumerable things you would never know about a patient. Things you had to learn to tolerate, to *stay with. Not knowing* and *staying with*—the buzzwords in her training.

"Apparently, his wife is convinced someone's stalking her," Joanna resumed. "Of course, as soon as I hear that, I have a hunch ..."

The next stretch of silence Gail endured by focusing on the crimson bud that, since last night, had nosed its way through the leaves in the flowerpot. Soon it will spurt blue pistils sticky with pollen, maybe tomorrow; at least some things one could predict. Patients come to you by word of mouth, she had been told. From whose mouth was the word to be issued? The whole thing was a mystery. Yet there must be many who would jump at the chance of unburdening themselves to an attentive stranger, someone who wouldn't bore them with her own stories. But how do you go about finding them—not that there was a shortage of melancholy faces about, though to discern inner turmoil from an unfortunate family trait was yet another

2

matter. Gail even considered placing a notice in the windows of local newsagents: *Anxiety, depression, relationship problems, self-esteem. Sex. Talking cure (for a nominal fee) by a keen student of human souls.*

"That hunch, Joanna. What was it?"

"Well! It's obvious, isn't it?" All of a sudden Joanna sounded impatient. "Clearly it's not *her*, the wife, who's afraid of being stalked, trailed, watched—whatever you call it."

"'You think it's him then? But watched by … whom?" As soon as she said it Gail wished she could take it back. Even she who didn't know much about politics was aware that for anyone coming from the ex-Eastern bloc, especially now with the war in Yugoslavia, the notion of being spied on wouldn't be so odd. He could be worried about Immigration. Or the secret police, or even some ethnic feud.

"With respect," Joanna snorted, and besides impatience there was now a sharper edge. "Shouldn't we think of this as his *presenting problem* first?"

How could she have missed it? Had she forgotten that whatever the patient brings, the therapist must consider as a mirror of his inner state? *Paranoia*, that's what Joanna is waiting for her to say. *Persecuting paranoia.* For once Gail had hit on the right answer.

"It can be tricky to shift paranoia," Joanna Wilson mused. "Tricky indeed. Perhaps someone like this ought to be seen by … well, by someone with more clinical experience. A psychiatrist perhaps."

Gail felt the receiver go clammy in her hand. Next to her Eddie's pyjamas lay neatly folded on the pillow as if waiting to be packed away and behind the window the sky loomed uniformly grey—not a shard of colour, a void. Was she now to watch her potential patient vanish into some obscure hospital department? So she mentioned her friend. A childhood friend who had developed a similar symptom to the Eastern European's; the delusion of being followed, secretly watched,

3

whatever Joanna Wilson wished to call it. And who had been treated with remarkable success not by drugs but by talking therapy.

"Well, that's unusual," Joanna said, though in her voice the hint of doubt remained.

Yes. In fact, Gail had kept in close contact with that friend, she told Joanna. And for a moment she believed that indeed there was this person, a good friend of hers who had given her a useful insight into such a condition. More than an insight— a method, really. She took another plunge. "In fact Joanna, looking in my diary I can pencil in the Eastern European for this coming Tuesday. At 3 p.m."

There followed another serving of silence and, on her part, another inspection of the potted plant. Gail had inherited it over twenty years ago—as long as that already? It came with a hidden note in their mother's spidery scrawl, tucked inside the lush leaves: *Will thrive on neglect but better on love.*

TWO

It was a balmy early autumn morning two weeks before the weather had turned, three weeks before Joanna Wilson's call. Cheapside, Milk Street, Wood Street, Gutter Lane ... Gail navigated through the warren of streets. Under her cardigan she wore only a short-sleeved dress. In the cafés the cabbies were mopping up the last of their fried breakfasts. Men in suits overtook her, trailing whiffs of aftershave, their damp hair like the feathers of freshly born chicks. Smartly dressed women in trainers strode past, swinging plastic bags containing a change of shoes. If she was to do well at the interview she too might soon slip into high heels in her own room in the Psychological Medicine Outpatient Department. If only her parents could see her.

The idea came from her supervisor. "What's this problem of no training patient, Gail? Every hospital grows a waiting list long as Great Wall in China." Rudi Chang's lips twitched in one of his teasing smiles. "They'll be happy to give you honorary post, you take a pick." Rudi clicked his delicate fingers, and indeed within a few days he had fixed her not one, but two hospital interviews.

She turned into Gresham Street. She was early, her appointment with Dr. Erica Field was at 9.30; once there she'd have time to find a quiet corner to brush up on a bit of theory. She was crossing Aldersgate Street when she noticed a wrought iron gate—a short cut. Through its bars her eyes met a strange sight: nestled between tall office buildings, a park swathed in a blanket of snow. A freak blizzard directly above this spot? In mid October? She opened the gate half expecting to bump against a painted board, a *trompe l'œil* blocking off a building site. But her sandals landed on snow. The lawn, the shrubs, the flowerbeds, everything around her was coated in white. On a yellow board black letters stated *Shooting In Progress*. An enchanted parallel world, surely a good omen; the snow was artificial but her luck today would be for real. The time before, her hands had shaken so violently she had to hide them. Though nerves weren't what had sunk her that time, it was something else. Something altogether unexpected. The man who had opened the door to her then, Dr. Burt Keech, was in his sixties. A towering figure: clear blue eyes, a leathery neck, white hair curling in the collar of his shirt. Broad-chested, with sturdy wrists. The instant she saw him she knew they had met before. But where?

To make space for her he shifted papers to the other end of the sofa. "Shall we start? Well then …" Dr. Burt Keech threw back his head, foraging in it for something, hopefully not too tricky. "Well then." He cleared his throat "What would you pay attention to during an initial assessment of a patient?"

What would she? History of mental illness in the family, related health problems, attempted suicides …

"Good! Very good." Drumming his fingers on the desk Dr. Keech smiled. "This of course you would have read in their file. But *you*, Miss May, what do *you* look for the first time you meet a patient?"

"Coherence of their story?"

He waited for more.

6

"Whether they are psychologically minded?"

"Yesss …? But isn't there something else you'd be mindful of?" His gaze explored her face. What could he be driving at? As if a plug had been pulled, her mouth felt suddenly drained.

"If …" she decided to dare him, "If I liked them?"

"Indeed! Your emotional response to the patient—what we call *countertransference*. Very important that. But what about the actual person in front of you?" His smile goaded her and just as she wondered if he had noticed that her forehead was now sticky with sweat, Dr. Keech leant forward and placed his large paw over her hand.

The effect on her was as bewildering as it was instantaneous. From then on her rational self remained only marginally there. The rest of her was taken by an irresistible urge to lie in Dr. Keech's arms, right there on the stained hospital carpet. To unbutton his shirt. To press her lips to the curly down on his chest; something poignant there, disarming, in men's body hair turning grey. A dull ache—the reliable barometer of the first stirs of arousal—shot through her left hip.

"The term I am referring to starts with T." Dr. Keech's voice reached her. "T for …?"

Could Dr. Keech mean the *truth*? If the truth be told, all of Gail's concentration was currently mobilised on not giving in to her incomprehensible impulse.

"T for … a tongue," she blurted out.

Not, of course, what Dr. Burt Keech had in mind. It was *transference* he was trying to tease out of her: transference— the transmission onto the therapist of deeply buried feelings we used to harbour for our mother or father. *Transference/ countertransference*—the concepts Rudi had simplified for her before she knew what anything meant, thus: "If your patient reports he's falling in love with you, don't go big-headed. Is not you Gail he fancies, is only *transference*. And if every night you dream erotically about him or her? There you have it—*countertransference*!"

Did her transference to Dr. Keech reveal an old Oedipal longing? A deep blush was working its way up her neck; one thing to speculate about the theory, another to find yourself lusting after a man of your father's age. And then she suddenly knew. Or rather it was her flesh that carried the memory of this unceremonious hand. If the doctor's palm weighing down hers shared her recall, nothing in his countenance showed.

Rudi Chang had phoned the next day: Burt had taken much pleasure in their "tête-à-tête". The interview had gone swimmingly, except for one small hiccup. The hiccup in question was that, according to Dr. Keech, Gail didn't possess the capacity to tolerate anxiety. Not when under pressure. Not yet. "What sort of pressure had Burt had in mind, Gail? Of being interviewed?"

She pretended not to understand what Rudi Chang meant.

"I see!" Her supervisor chuckled. "The old hunk's laid it on, isn't it? I should've warned you."

Despite her spiky hairdo and restless eyes, Dr. Erica Field—"Please call me Erica"—turned out to be a warm creature. "Tell me, what makes a librarian want to retrain as a psychotherapist?"

"I only work part-time," Gail put her right. One of Dr. Erica's eyes settled on her while the other scanned the ceiling. "I always liked psychology. My parents were both doctors. We had Freud's books at home."

Dr. Erica signalled approval.

Encouraged, Gail went on. "I read his case histories like they were novels. I went through them all. In my early teens. I suppose it was at that time I had discovered how to intensify words."

Erica's wayward eye joined the first to glare at her, "Intensify words? Tell me more."

8

"Oh it was just a game." Already she regretted saying too much. "It was nothing, really."

"Game? What sort of a game?"

She remembered her parents discussing someone with a similarly bulging, similarly unpredictable gaze: an overactive thyroid had been mentioned. Other problems went with it—depression for one. She felt a surge of instant sympathy towards Dr. Field, towards Erica. "Basically, the trick was to make each syllable resonate in me."

A rapid back and forth of Dr. Field's gaze. "How?"

"For example I'd feel it here." Gail opened to Dr. Erica her palms. "Or I'd curl my lips over the tips of my teeth. I guess these days I might think of it as oral libidinal cathexis."

"Gosh! You *have* read your Freud, haven't you."

Gail hadn't really thought about any of this, not at that age or ever since. So why on earth to pick this moment? But what was done was done. Thankfully she retained enough sense not to dwell on how the words had erupted in the moist warmth of her mouth; how she used to touch with her tongue the soft hair above her upper lip, drop the book and wait for the dull delicious pain to spread from her hip to her belly. And further down.

"Any other reasons for becoming a therapist?"

She thought of all the valid reasons she could supply. A calling. A wish to help. An urge to alleviate suffering. But Dr. Erica with her three o'clock, nine o'clock gaze and her penchant for depression deserved better than that. The least Gail could do was to be frank. So she said, "To find out who I am." This sounding too sloppy, she added, "I guess I want to help myself."

"As good a reason as any," Dr. Erica said. "In this profession we all have something to heal. You can start next week."

"But Dr. Field, Erica …" So sudden was her good fortune that she wanted to deserve it better. "You didn't ask me anything about the theory."

9

Dr. Erica's eyes quizzed her comically. "Should I? What for, dear?"

Gail gushed something about how grateful she felt to be given this chance. "The only small matter," she told Erica, "is that the patient you're going to allocate to me, *my training patient* who I immensely look forward to working with, will have to be supervised by my own supervisor. A rule on my course. I hope you and your department won't object."

"*A training patient*?" Dr. Field's raised brows indicated her career stretched too far back to remember this early but necessary stage in any therapist's genesis. "I'm sorry but I've never mentioned a *training patient*." The confusion began to unravel. Dr. Field had assumed Gail had been told that before she could treat outpatients, who by the way were not suitable as training patients, she would have to attend regular hospital rounds. "For six months. That's the rule, dear."

Now it was Gail's turn to be puzzled. "Hospital rounds?"

"Yes, on a psychiatric ward. To give you a chance to meet some more seriously disturbed members of the public." Dr. Erica's eyes danced, each to its own tune. "Useful this, dear. In case one day a psychopath turns up at the doorstep of your private practice. Then you'll know the signs and bale out."

THREE

Joanna Wilson had called later the same day. "The Eastern European accepted the session on Tuesday, at 3 p.m. But Gail, no going back on this I'm afraid," she warned. Having conceded that, after all, the man's paranoia might pose a valuable challenge to a student in her third year of training already, Joanna explained that, regrettably, the bit of the paper where she had scribbled the fellow's name and all the rest had vanished into thin air. "Builders' mess!"

On Saturday, Eddie helped Gail to unscrew the bed. They reassembled it in the room upstairs which the shared wall with Ben's hi-fi had made redundant. But this would have to change. Her old bedroom, with its easy access from the street, was to become her consulting room. Then Eddie went to his Vauxhall flat to work on his designs and she spent the rest of the day rolling fresh paint onto the walls.

On Sunday she retouched the skirting boards, polished the floor and buffed the window. Next day, after work, in a bout of late-night shopping, she purchased two red leather armchairs—the first serious pieces of furniture she had ever bought. And a rug that was like velvet under her feet. She felt like a parent preparing a room for a newborn, though who that newborn was, whether she or her patient, she couldn't tell.

11

While searching for a therapist for herself she had noticed that more often than not, therapy was practised among pieces of discarded furniture in underheated rooms. The idea of lying on one of those musty couches, exposing her innermost self to someone whose idea of warmth was a smelly oil heater, made the whole prospect unpalatable. When the time came, she had promised herself, her own consulting room would be different.

On Tuesday morning she dragged Ben out of bed to help her lug a couch in from the basement. Befuddled by sleep, Ben staggered around. "Mum! Why don't you ask Ed?" When she replied that Eddie was in Vauxhall, Ben said, "I just wish you'd quit calling him that." She pretended not to understand. "Eddie—Benny? Geddit?" He glared at her. "Like Ed was my dad or something."

The plants came next. From various corners of the house she brought them in, pot by pot. When the room acquired the air of a funeral parlour she reduced them to two. On the wall she hung a reproduction of Frida Kahlo's *Itzculinty Dog with Me* in which Frida sat on a chair gazing mysteriously past a miniscule creature on spindly legs. Gail loved the straightness of Frida's neck and the calmness of her crossed hands. Eddie said the picture reminded him of her. It surprised her: she never thought of herself as headstrong as Frida, quite the opposite. Then, seeing the sky dim with clouds, she replaced stern Frida with a seaside watercolour Eddie had painted on one of their holidays.

The next thing was to decide how she and her patient were to face one another. Would eyeball to eyeball be too direct? She shuffled the chairs back and forth, taking turns in each, till she arranged them half facing the wall and half each other. To herself she allocated the chair opposite the door. It did cross her mind that sitting by the door might be safer if … but she stifled the idea. Not the right moment to spook yourself. By her elbow she put a clock with numerals large enough to see at a glance. Whenever she passed the couch she slid her fingers over its roughly woven fabric. But she was not about to invite her new patient to lie down. Not for now. Though in the not too distant future she saw herself—and when she imagined it her heart lurched—sitting behind a reclining patient in the same pose Phyllis Horobin had adopted, twice a week, behind the crown of her own head.

Phyllis Horobin, her role model. Phyllis and the theory; volumes and volumes of it, dense and awe-inspiring, not rhyming yet not unlike poetry. Some read more like Greek tragedies. Before too long, Gail hoped, those grand concepts would become her companions, her helpers. If anyone were to ask her how psychotherapy worked she struggled for the right words. How do you convey something so intricate, so elusive you can hardly grasp it yourself? Now, in an hour or so, it will be up to her, her alone to make the whole thing slot into place. Whenever she glanced out and caught sight of a passer-by leaning into the wind she imagined it was her patient turning up early. The Eastern European with no name, no land, not even a phone number attached to him. Not yet. With the falling of the first raindrops she started to worry about the new chairs. Were they likely to stain? Perhaps she should have gone for black rather than burgundy. And what about tears? Tears were to be expected. But from a man? She placed a fresh box of paper hankies at hand, just in case.

At twenty to three she checked the room for the last time. Eddie's watercolour seemed suitably understated. She wiped clean the answering machine in the eventuality of an important message and went upstairs to change. At dawn, after rereading once more the chapter about paranoia, she had laid out her clothes: the dark green top she had only worn to parties, an embroidered mauve jacket, black slacks, ankle boots.

The doorbell rang while she was putting on mascara. Her watch showed eleven minutes to three. She did make it clear to Joanna Wilson that, in the absence of a waiting room, her

13

patient was to arrive exactly on the dot. But since this was their very first meeting and since outside the sky was lit by lightning and the rain was bowing the tree branches like some drowned woman's hair, there was nothing for it but to let him in.

She opened the door to two figures huddling under a semi-collapsed umbrella, the ground around them boiling with water eruptions. At first glance she took them to be a father with a teenage daughter. The man's stoop—a comical genuflection to keep the umbrella close to the girl's head—suggested a dad protecting his cherished daughter. Though his wiry figure and coarse hair were nothing like the girl's roundness, her moonlike face framed by a bob.

"Can I help you?"

The girl's eyes shifted to the man who, ready to explain their business, bared his teeth. The next moment there was a flash and the man was suddenly skidding about as if learning to skate. To steady him the girl extended her arm but only caught the umbrella. Then the air around them exploded and Gail was flung against the doorframe. When she opened her eyes again the man was on the ground, the lashings of water turning his purple shirt into a sodden shroud. "Tomaashee?" The woman—now Gail saw that she was a woman not a girl, it was her fringe that gave her an air of someone younger—called through the trumpet she made out of her fingers. "Tomaashee!"

The man sprang up and trapped Gail's hand in a wet squeeze. "Thomas Smutny. You must be Miss May, the psychotherapist."

Not a stranger from the street then, this man was to be her patient. He stood so close to her that his wet ribs nearly grazed her breasts. From the ridge of his nose a few hairs were sprouting. To spend a whole hour with this man, just him and her alone, suddenly seemed an intolerable prospect. He wouldn't take long to spot who she was: a part-time librarian in her middle years, half a dozen semi-digested psycho-books her only tool.

14

"Hope we didn't cause you any fright." The man grinned at her. "Hell out there, isn't it? I brought you my wife Alenka."

His wife. What was she supposed to do with her? Surely he doesn't expect her to invite them both in. For such an eventuality her training had not prepared her. "I'm very sorry," she said, sounding kind but firm. "I know it's raining but I don't have a waiting room. So I'm afraid your wife will have to ..." She vaguely gestured behind them to where a brown brook was running noisily into the gutter.

"Oh, not to worry. I'm sure my wife won't mind me sitting in. Will you, Alenka?" The woman shook her head, causing droplets of water to trickle from her fringe down her full cheeks.

Sitting in. His foreigner's English? And then it dawned on her: Joanna Wilson got it wrong, it wasn't Thomas whatever his name was who was coming to see her, it was his wife.

"I'm afraid," Gail said, "individual therapy takes place only one to one."

"One to one?"

"Yes, without exceptions." She made her voice solid against the patter of the rain. "And without witnesses." The word *witnesses* made it sound as if something untoward might take place. From now on, she thought, I need to consider every word. To speed up the proceedings she stepped inside and held the door.

The man hesitated, murmured something in his wife's wet hair. She listened, never ceasing to monitor the street. Till her husband gently prodded her forward. "All right then. She's all yours."

She eyed the young woman in front of her: A-len-ka. Mid- to late thirties, stumpy, yet not unattractive. Round face, oily skin. Dewy. Small, delicate mouth. Brown eyes that soaked in each detail. Her bob, the wig-like coiffure dyed the colour of honey and kept in place by lacquer, made her resemble an

15

old-fashioned doll. A childlike face above prominent breasts, a pink shirt pushed into a school uniform-type navy blue skirt, too short to hide her chubby thighs; flat laced-up shoes—the whole get-up more like a camouflage. The soles of Alenka's shoes had already left damp imprints on the beige carpet. To protect the chair Gail threw over it a woollen rug. All along she refrained from making small talk. She noticed that Alenka kept her left arm awkwardly pressed to her breasts.

"Something wrong with your arm?"

Instead of a response a blank stare. Much disputed—a moment like this. Some believe the first hour should be no more than ticking off a list: progenitors, partners, siblings … Some go as far as sketching a family tree. According to Gail's training, however, the first session had to be no different to any other therapeutic hour: offer no niceties, no leading questions, work solely with what the client brings. Go easy on smiling.

She watched Alenka's eyes dart around the walls; her patient was a woman after all—an unexpected piece of luck! But how long were you supposed to stick to silence? Every second of which was loudly marked by the new clock; too late to get rid of it now. And how was Alenka to know where to start?

Gail decided to give her a cue: "Here you can speak about anything. Anything you want. Naturally, whatever you tell me is totally confidential."

Naturally, not the best choice; nothing natural about laying yourself open to a stranger, especially if you came from Alenka's part of the world. There wasn't just the war; it had been three, four years since the wave of revolutions swept Eastern Europe. From under her fringe Alenka's gaze reached the window, then briskly pulled away. Something disturbing in those branches? Or is it her fear of being watched? Alenka's eyes had found Eddie's watercolour and there they stayed. Widening. Drinking the picture. Maybe Gail should have left the wall blank.

"This is painted where?"

Finally, her patient had spoken. So thrilled was Gail to hear Alenka's voice that she had to hold herself back from volunteering a detailed description of the particular beach on the island of Krk where Eddie had set up his folding chair and his paints. But this was therapy, not a friendly chat. She suggested it might be more useful if Alenka, "If I may call you that," told her what the picture brought to *her* mind.

"My name is Alena," her patient corrected her. "Alena Sokol."

A-le-na So-kol. Gail silently rehearsed the name, the surname sounding somewhat different to her husband's. Alenka must be a form of endearment. Still no progress with the picture. That particular swell of the waves, that stretch of the sky; did it remind Alena of home perhaps? Minutes ticked away. The damp stains on Alena's shirt were evaporating. Now and then she gave her right arm a slow, thoughtful rub. And each time a tangy aroma reached Gail's nostrils, as though from a musk deer's secret gland. "I'm sorry, I should've asked for your name first. Would you like to tell me something about yourself? Or maybe why you want to start therapy?"

Even before she had finished Gail knew she'd got it wrong again: she had forced on Alena her own questions, and two at once. A sure recipe for not getting an answer. Yet, this time Alena Sokol rose to the challenge.

"London Transport," she announced. "I work for."

Victory! Gail was right to spot something of a uniform. She envisaged a heaving early morning platform, Alena Sokol blowing a whistle. A lonely figure amid the silent multitudes; not much chance to practise the finer points of your English.

"London Transport! That must be very interesting!" *Very interesting?* In less than half an hour this monosyllabic woman had turned her into an imbecile. Suddenly, Gail's mind was blank, totally blank. As if her years of study counted for nothing.

"My other question, the one about starting therapy—"

"I don't want te-ra-py," Alena Sokol interrupted her. "Tomash wants it." Was this all Alena had to say? A tide of fatigue swept over Gail. Not very likely that she'd manage to hold onto this poor woman marshalled here by her husband. To be approved as her training patient she'd need to be coming for a year and a half, minimum. Best to get it over with quickly. "No one can force you to have therapy," she instructed Alena from her smart new chair. By now Alena was clawing frantically at her arm as though a colony of ants had invaded her sleeve. "There *is* something wrong with your arm, isn't there?"

With the help of her other hand Alena Sokol lifted the limb in question and glared at it as if it were a sick infant. Her eyes became glazed; drops of sweat had gathered on her nose. Then she gagged. The next, deeper surge catapulted her to her feet.

"The toilet's on the right!" Gail called after her, in time she hoped. She listened for what was happening behind the wall. But all she heard was the scratch of rain and the chime of a passing ice cream van. Was Alena being sick? Had she fainted? It suddenly occurred to Gail that in that moment Alena had touched the metal umbrella handle her arm might have been struck by lightning. Could anyone survive such a thing?

When Alena Sokol returned, a wad of bunched toilet paper held to her mouth, Gail's further enquiries were met with a mute stare. Yet, the way Gail now saw it, her qualification depended on making this woman talk. And keeping her talking, twice a week, until the next but one spring. Outside, the gusts of wind hurled water against the windowpanes. Gail got up and turned on the table light. She had to pin down the times of Alena Sokol's therapy slots around her shifts.

It transpired, though later Gail could not recall Alena's exact words, that she kept ordinary office hours. No foggy dawns or chilly nights for her: in fact she clocked in at the London Transport Lost Property office at ten and clocked out at five. Gail suggested they met on Tuesdays at 6.30 after Alena's work

18

and on Fridays at eight in the morning. She explained that the therapeutic hour consists of fifty minutes only. As for the fee, she had made up her mind to charge the absolute minimum: money was of no import, having a patient was. Could Alena Sokol manage five pounds? In the absence of an answer she wrote the amount down for her, next to the times when they were to meet.

At ten to four she stood up. "The session is over." Obediently Alena Sokol also rose. That was when Gail noticed something glistening on her elbow. "Excuse me, you've got something here." She peeled off what turned out to be a razor blade, the same as Eddie used; she registered that it gave slight resistance. Slight but strong enough for her fingers to have to tug at it. As if Alena Sokol was a walking magnet.

FOUR

She returned the blade to the shelf in the bathroom from where, probably due to static electricity, it had adhered itself to Alena's elbow. The air was steamy as if during her brief stay Alena had run off gallons of water, and there was an unfamiliar whiff. A fly was buzzing on the outside of the lavatory bowl feeding on a tiny orange-coloured flake. Gail scraped it off and inspected it on her finger: a piece of retched carrot? Sweet pepper? She sprayed the toilet with cleaner and scrubbed the washbasin. If she had the energy she would get out the Hoover and tackle the carpet. Anything but sitting down to write her notes. What was there to report besides the mix-up about who was coming to see her and Alena Sokol's nausea? Or that after the session her patient had strolled out without turning or saying goodbye, and that only then did Gail remember that in her keenness to behave to protocol she had never got round to asking Alena for her address and phone number. She felt a hopeless failure.

"How did your lesson go?" Eddie was about to disappear into the kitchen where she heard a cork pop. Who cared it was called a *session*, she was glad Eddie was back. They had met over a decade ago when his fingers lingered on hers a little longer while returning an overdue book. Edward Berg—a lecturer in graphic design. To Gail everything about Eddie seemed flaw-less: the symmetry of his flaxen moustache, the blue veins on his arms delicate as porcelain patterns; the silky ash-blond down on his buttocks; his seashell-pink penis. Even his habit of wetting his whiskers with his tongue mesmerised her. The fine proportions of his boyish face made hers feel assembled in a somewhat slapdash manner.

Eddie reappeared balancing two champagne flutes. "Here's to Fraulein Freud! Prost!" Foreign accents not quite being Eddie's forte but Gail laughed all the same. The fizz went straight to her head. Slapdash: that's what her session with Alena Sokol had been. Wishing to forget the whole thing she took Eddie's hand and laid it on her breast. He leant over and found her mouth. And she wanted to stay like this forever: not moving, not saying anything. Then Eddie went back to the kitchen to fetch the tray with the dinner plates: quinoa, greens, salad with alfalfa sprouts ... everything, just so. The dessert was to be a surprise.

On the news, somewhere in the Balkans—Bosnia, Croatia?—a woman in black was telling the camera in sharp tones how she had stumbled across the body of her husband: shot on the porch. Then she found her daughter: sprawled across the kitchen threshold. And finally her youngest: hacked in his bed, a boy of eleven. Eddie laid his fork down. "We don't have to watch this while we eat, do we?"

Gail would have liked to let Eddie know it was not entirely implausible that the patient who had sat in her room just a few hours ago had come from this part of the world. But there was confidentiality to be observed. So she made do with, "Let's just see what's going on there."

They had gone to Croatia for a holiday because of its unspoiled beaches. Yet it was the roughly paved seaside path above the rocks where she had asked Eddie to admire the sun-set that Gail would never forget. When they turned back Ben, only four at the time, was gone. Only an instant before, he had been padding in front of them and now the path was empty. They shouted, they ran here and there till they spotted his little shape, flung under the jutting rocks. She can still see the holidaymakers' faces gaping at the gash on Ben's forehead as they raced through the wood, Eddie carrying Ben in his arms, the pine needles cracking under their feet. A man offered them a lift in his car to the nearby hospital. When they apologised for the blood on his white fake fur he waved his hand. He had a handsome, tanned smile. Muslim? Serb? Croat? It didn't make any difference, the war was yet to come.

On the screen a woman in a headscarf hurled stones at a passing truck. "You bastards! You killed my son! My son!" she yelled at the terrified faces peering from under the canvas. Who were they? Muslims or Croats? Eddie got up to take away their empty plates. Having swum in their sea, having trusted their nurses and blabbered tearful thanks to their surgeon for stitching up Ben's head, they couldn't grasp why this war had begun and still had no more than a hazy notion of where to locate these people on a map.

"I'm his mother," the woman screamed. "You killed him and you won't even give me his body back! F**k you! F**k you," duly the subtitles translated. "F**k your mother through her mouth!"

Then Eddie came back carrying a frying pan ablaze with blue flames. They were having flambé bananas. "Ta-daa!"

By the time she turned the dishwasher on it was midnight. Still no sign of Ben. In the new bedroom upstairs, Eddie was asleep stretched on his back, arms by his sides. The pharaoh pose, he called it. And she, like an orchid thriving on little but air, slithered one leg under his and with the other entwined his thighs. Her arms echoed the arrangement. In her old bedroom the bursts of traffic and snippets of conversations from the street had made her feel close to life's hub. But here, at the back of the house, at this hour the only sound to break the night was an occasional shriek. Of laughter or of terror, she couldn't tell which. At around two she got up and tiptoed downstairs. In her new consulting room, the shadows made a quivering projection on the wall—she used to watch these before falling asleep. She pulled an armchair to the window, her thoughts turned to Alena Sokol. Where was she? Asleep next to Thomas? Or awake, thinking her thoughts? If, indeed, Yugoslavia was where she came from, had she ever been on such a truck, ever witnessed such scenes? What would she find to talk about to someone who knew nothing of war and its casualties?

The church bell struck three just as a car pulled up— a trusted minicab driver returning her son to her! Gail watched the car sitting there with the engine running. Craning her neck she made out a man's hand resting on the gearstick. What were they waiting for? Perhaps Ben didn't have enough money for the fare. She should get her purse. Or maybe this wasn't a cab at all and the man was some pervert who had picked up Ben in a pub. Should she pull the window open and shout? Before she could make up her mind the car pulled away.

With every purr of an approaching car she felt a surge of hope. Each receding engine filled her with despair. Nothing to worry about, Ben is with friends, she repeated to herself. Yet in her head the refrain kept on: *Why did you delete Ben's message from the answering machine? What if you'll never hear his voice again?*

When Ben finally strode in he found her leaning against the kitchen counter with a cup in her hand. "Hi mum. Why aren't you in bed?" He lifted the lid from the pan. "Bolognese, yum!"

Eddie being a vegetarian she always prepared something else for Ben. She watched him scoop cold mouthfuls straight from the saucepan. She passed him a plate, but he ignored it. In recent months Ben had shot up. The way he held himself, how he tossed his hair from his forehead, she could have been looking at Benny. Benny, his young dad of whom Ben had no memory. She asked Ben where he had been but he continued twisting the fork. You'll be exhausted at school tomorrow, she said. Why didn't you phone?

"I did. But the phone's kaput."

The injustice of it all appalled her: it was because of him she couldn't sleep and now this. "You liar! You've just made it up!"

"Mum!" Ben yanked the receiver from its base and rammed it to her ear. And indeed, it was dead. Ben poured himself a glass of water, drained it in one loud gulp and strolled out, leaving the fork stuck in the pot.

FIVE

In the three years Gail had been coming she had never seen Mrs. Horobin on her feet. The first time she rang the bell at 99 Stillness Road the door had opened by itself: *Gail May? Do let yourself in!* Even before Gail had met her, Phyllis Horobin's sonorous voice had called her by her full name. No one but her father, and even he only in rare moments, had ever addressed her by both names. So it was that her first sighting of Mrs. Horobin had been through a haze of tears. Normally, she didn't cry in front of others. But with Phyllis Horobin it was as though she had reserved her tears for her. Phyllis and this room with its liver-red walls, dusty green curtains, and shelves crowded with miniature cacti.

The training stipulated they each see their own therapist with the same frequency they saw their training patients. As always Horobin let her in by pressing the button on her armrest. Not only could Gail not picture her standing or walking, she could not picture her anywhere else but sunk deep in her green velvet armchair. Mrs. Horobin was in her late seventies, the age Gail's parents, had they lived, would have now reached. Over the past year Horobin's interpretations had grown slower, her pauses lengthier. It worried Gail. Had Phyllis fallen asleep behind her? Should she turn and look?

With the exception of a cat she sometimes sensed behind the door, she never heard anyone else.

Before lowering herself onto the couch she tried to extend the time she could see Horobin's soft cheeks. They made her think of the almond pastries dusted in vanilla sugar her mother used to buy in an Italian shop in Dulwich. When Mrs. Horobin smiled, her eyes disappeared behind her thick lenses. Her swollen feet, stuffed into soft leather shoes, she kept propped up on a small upholstered stool; her body wrapped in loosely knitted cardigans.

Today Gail didn't know where to start. She stared at the tasselled lampshade by the foot of the couch. Till now it had never struck her how ugly it was; in fact the whole room was shabby. Suddenly, she felt annoyed. More than annoyed, angry. She stuck to her silence, kept it longer than ever before.

"I saw my parent," she said eventually.

"Your parent? Was it in a dream?"

"No, not my parent, my *patient*. I meant to say I saw my patient."

A Freudian slip. In her head, no doubt, Horobin has already made a clever link, though Gail for the life of her couldn't guess what it could be. For a start, her parents were both dead. Daddy was the first. One day he failed to show up at a meeting. When he didn't come home in the evening they contacted the police. In those times you didn't carry around plastic cards embossed with your name: it took days to trace him. A fatal heart attack in a part of town where no one knew him. With Mummy it was worse: not even a year later they had opened her up to remove a cyst. Before promptly closing her again. As a doctor Mother knew what it meant. And there was nothing for Gillie and Gail, her two girls, to say, or do. Nothing but to watch her fade. Once Gail had gathered courage to ask, "Mummy, what will I do without you?" Her mother's reply came back without hesitation: "A lot, I hope."

Today, Phyllis Horobin's chesty inhalations sounded maddeningly loud. "Oh, so you now have a patient."

"Yes. And it was a disaster." Gail twisted her head to look behind. "Mrs. Horobin, what if I just lay here and never said a word? What would you do?"

"I'd try to find out why."

"Well, you haven't, just now. Have you?" Her voice came out harsher than she had wished. "I wonder for how long you'd let me stew."

"I wonder if you're angry with me."

"With you? What for?"

"For abandoning you in your silence," Mrs. Horobin suggested quietly. "Perhaps you had hoped that I'd rescue you from it."

To let Horobin know how absurd her interpretation was Gail forced air through her nostrils. "I expect no one to rescue me. And no one ever does!" She heard her voice faltering, thinning.

From behind, Horobin calmly placed a box of paper tissues by her head. "I think you're still angry with your parents for having abandoned you, Gail May."

Ridiculous! With her elbow she knocked the tissues off, as if by mistake. These days Horobin's ways infuriated her. "They haven't abandoned me—they died." Phyllis Horobin made it sound as if they ran off on a whim.

On the way to supervision she stopped by a phone booth to call BT. We're sending someone round in the afternoon, she was told. She managed to get hold of Eddie to ask him to wait for them. Then she parked outside Rudi Chang's house. She still had a few minutes. She took out her *Dictionary of Psychodynamic Psychotherapy*. The *paranoid-schizoid position* means, she read, that you find your destructive impulses in others. That's exactly what happened at Horobin's: she had her paranoid event of believing that not only her mother and father, but Benny too, the whole world had abandoned her. The way out of *paranoid-schizoid* was to shift yourself to another place where you accept those bad thoughts as your very own, the theory said. Oddly, this more desirable place went under the name *the depressive position*.

My anger is mine, I own it, she instructed herself as she tackled Rudi Chang's rusty gate. She reiterated the same during her encounter with a prickly bush that had toppled across the path to his front door and the clump of reeds that mopped her face as if she were in a car wash. She rang the bell.

"Coming! Coming!" She heard Rudi's falsetto. And then Gustav's howling, backed by a chorus of operatic voices. She zipped up her bag. Once, while she left it unguarded, Rudi's black Doberman had pulled out her salami sandwich and swallowed it in one go. She heard a brief scuffle, the howling receded, the door opened, and Rudi Chang beamed at her, his egg-like skull smooth and shiny. Over a black T-shirt he wore a pink brocade waistcoat. "In previous incarnation my boy was a singer, I'm telling you, Gail."

Barking behind the kitchen door escorted them to Rudi's consulting room with its couch, chairs, even the ceiling candelabra draped in multicoloured fabrics. Light struggled in through a pattern of star stickers on the garden door. The worn armchair received her with a whine; a spring dug in her buttock.

"Congratulations!" Skilfully wedging himself between the writing desk and a filing cabinet with overspilling drawers that wouldn't close Rudi looked at her expectantly. "I already heard from Jo-Anna. What is his name?"

She explained her client was not a man.

"So! A-le-na!" Rudi clicked his lips. "A-le-na who? Sou-kol?!" He scrawled it in his large notepad. "Now Gail, perchance," he cocked his skull, "you enquired how old Sou-kol is?"

She shook her head.

28

"No problem, guaranteed to pop out later. Or is it pop up? After all those years …" Rudi Chang's small soft hand drew an ellipse in the air. "You written your session up, haven't you."

Rudi Chang had arrived in London from China via Hong Kong with two goals: to study Jungian psychoanalysis and to own a dog, apparently both something of a rarity back home. There might have been other reasons of which Gail knew nothing. While Rudi carefully scrawled a line down the middle of a page dividing it in two, she produced her meagre notes. "Please start, Gail. I'm all ears."

"Well. Alena comes in and sits down."

"No! No! Please Gail!" Rudi halted her. "Is important to start from first impression of our patient, the very first."

"OK, there is a thunderstorm."

"A thunderstorm?" Rudi chuckled.

"I open the door to a man and a woman. They're both drenched. The man whom I take to be the woman's father slips and falls—"

"Let's pause here," Rudi stopped her again. "So—there is a deluge. A father falls. A faa-llen faa-ther …," he hummed through his nose. "Perhaps we're in for … Oedipal issues." From their tight corners his eyes checked her. "Please carry on, Gail."

"Alena comes in, sits down. She is wet from the rain." Uhum … uhum … Rudi jotted something in the left column. "She keeps quiet so I ask her why she wants to start therapy and she says it is not her who wants it, it is Thomas." The lightning and the sore arm she left out, they sounded too improbable.

"Who's Thomas?"

"That man who came with her, her husband."

"So we know he is not her papa but her husband."

"Yes. I already knew this from Joanna Wilson."

"Uhum. Do you remember how she said it?"

"Joanna?"

"No." Rudi checked in his pad. "Sou-kol. How she said she doesn't want therapy."

"I don't vont te-rapy," Gail impersonated her patient.

Rudi tapped his pencil on the page and said that next time she should write her notes verbatim. She stared at her paper. She had offended him, she who had never managed to learn another language.

"And your A-le-na, she's coming from ...?"

"Eastern Europe." She kept her head bowed.

"Eastern Europe, ocho! More than one land in Eastern Europe, isn't it."

For a few minutes they remained silent, listening to Gustav's distant growling. "So what happened next?"

"Well ... really, not much."

"Sou-kol's parents still living?"

She shrugged.

"And children? Sou-kol has any?"

Oh no, no children. On this she was definite. In spite of her full breasts and wide hips she could see nothing maternal in Alena.

"So after Miss Sou-kol tells you she doesn't want therapy ..."

She frantically searched for what to say. "I asked Alena if ... if she feels that she must go along with what others expect of her. You know, because of what Thomas had said to her."

Visibly impressed, Rudi looked up. "You returning Sou-kol's projection back to her. Excellent!" He quickly scribbled in both columns. "And Miss Sou-kol?" He waited, his small lips parted as if anticipating something tasty.

She pretended to examine her notes. What would Alena have said had Gail pointed out her compliance with her husband? Had she thought of it there and then? Maybe Alena would have remembered an incident, something from childhood for instance, about having to please someone, even if it meant doing something she didn't want to. And then? Then this could have led to them thinking why this was so. In short it could have led to what Gail was training for, to therapy. To Rudi she said that Alena just kept silent.

"Silent. Uhum. For how long?"

She shrugged again.

"So who is breaking silence? Gail or Miss Sou-kol?" How much longer will she have to carry on with this charade? "Gail?" Rudi gently brought her back. "By the way Gail, we still missing something. Something important." Another nod of encouragement. She thought of her fiasco with Dr. Keech and felt her forehead glisten. "We're missing Sou-kol's presenting problem, isn't it?"

"Oh sorry, I forgot. Alena thinks she's being stalked. Followed."

"Followed!" Rudi jotted down something on the left side of the page. "By whom?" He held his pen poised in the air.

She admitted that, unfortunately, this didn't come up in the session. It was Joanna Wilson who told her.

Rudi sighed and poked his ear with his pen. "You know Gail, something makes me think this *following business* Sou-kol using as decoy." He smiled at her impishly. "How do you say? Red herring?"

Generous of Rudi to try to humour her, to pull her out of a tight spot. Now it was her turn to offer something back. She told Rudi Alena Sokol had told her that she works in the London Transport Lost Property office.

"Ocho!" Rudi perked up again. He drummed his thigh. "Gail, already I'm intrigued by your Miss Sou-kol. And your interpretation?"

"My interpretation?"

"Of her workplace."

She stared back in her notes: it hadn't occurred to her to interpret where Alena worked. What's wrong with her? If she can't remember that her job is to analyse everything as unconscious communication, what is she doing here?

"Sorry Rudi." She stood up stuffing her notes in the bag. "It was a washout, a complete washout. I've been making it all up." She tried to squeeze past him but Rudi caught her elbow.

"She not working in Lost and Found?"

"No, it's not that. It's … simply … I'm not cut out for this."

"Gail! Please!" Rudi led her back to her chair. "Nobody born a therapist, we all learning." He patted her hand. "Together we can think why you don't ask. Something you picking from Sou-kol? This only a first session, Gail." He returned to his chair and across the room held her in his gaze. "So. Your Sou-kol works in Lost Property and she suffered many losses: her homeland, her history, her language … this we already know. But this, Gail, makes her an *en-thra-lling* patient." He saw her pulling a grimace. "Yes, *en-thra-lling*. Because Sou-kol works not only in a place of loss. But also in a place of finding. And for your patient," Rudi Chang lifted both his hands as if to embrace the air, "this may gesture hope. Yes, Gail—hope. That one day Sou-kol can *mourn* her losses."

Mourning: another buzzword in their training. Mourning that is with us from the moment we peek out between our mother's thighs. Already then we mourn not being able to swim back in her sweet safe waters. And this is only the first chapter.

"No sooner we spread our toast with plum jam we mourning, Gail." Rudi inflated his silky cheeks. "Mourning—the absence … of … marmalade!" In his face the quivering balloons popped, inviting her to join in. And deep in the house Gustav's joyful howl announced that the fifty minutes of supervision were finally over.

From Rudi Chang she drove straight to Manor Hall, a Gothic revival residence built by a nineteenth-century industrialist where her training kept rooms on permanent hire. On the way, she usually pulled up by a corner shop to treat herself to a sesame bar. The next hour and a half were her favourite: she parked the car in a side street of Thirties houses, of quaint turrets and pagoda roofs. She read theory papers, ate her provisions, and watched the street lanterns flicker to life. In winter she kept the windows shut to conserve the warmth. When the days grew longer she rolled them down to sniff the air. Sometimes she dozed off. If it rained she watched the water rivulets racing down the misty glass. She thought of these moments as mini-holidays.

Today she passed the shop without stopping. There was a respite in the rain but everything seemed coated in slimy grey; here and there the gloom was lifted by a colourful patch of leaves, as if someone had hurled a bucket of paint on them in a violent fit. She parked the car. What took place at Rudi's felt bad enough and now she was about to face her peers. At five minutes to five Karla Urbanova's blonde ponytail swung into her rear-view mirror, armed with a briefcase in each hand, one for paper clips, highlighting pens and various stationary, the other for books and papers.

Karla, with her doctorate in economy from Prague University, she feared most. Karla who spent the whole of their first year insisting that the Czech language didn't have a word for *anxiety*: no, Czechs simply had no use for something so vague. Admittedly, she had adjusted her views since, though she continued to battle other issues: the absence of formal lectures, the intellectually slack seminars for which no one came properly prepared. Wasn't this supposed to be a postgraduate study? Peer learning, what was this for? The lame leading the blind, it seemed like. And the fees they had to pay! Even under communism the academic standard was superior, by far. If anyone was to spot Gail's blunders it was Karla Urbanova.

As soon as the heavy wooden door closed after Karla, Gail turned the ignition on again and, checking that no one was about, started to roll away from the curb. In the morning, providing the phone works, she will ring Miranda Green, their tutor, and blame her absence on a migraine. She was in the middle of her manoeuvre when the car shook as if a boulder had landed on its roof.

"Right! Gailie spin the wheel to the right!" Nigel Whale grimaced at her through the window. "Now left! Towards me!" He directed her, his carrot hair smudging his forehead, freckles crawling over his gums, around his small teeth. "Superb!" Giving her a thumbs-up Nigel yanked the door open.

The news about her patient had already reached her tribe: four in their year in total. With its somewhat hazy career prospects the Institute struggled to recruit new candidates. So how did she get on? They were all keen to know. She started with Alena Sokol's name. Then she told them about Thomas whom Alena called *Tomashee*. And that they were from somewhere in Eastern Europe.

"Excuse me Gail," Karla Urbanova said, her hair pulled back so tight that the corners of her eyes were stretched, like a cat's, "but no one's from *somewhere*. They're from Czech Republic as they now call it, after our Slovak brothers decided to split." How did Karla know? From their names, of course!

To mask her embarrassment Gail launched into Alena Sokol's obdurate silence, her nausea, her throwing up. Alena's fear of being stalked she left out, for the lack of any further details. While talking she tried to recall what she knew about Karla Urbanova's country: a revolution. And an invasion. Or were they the same thing? And that a student set fire to himself, in protest. There was something shockingly stubborn in his self-sacrificing act; it reminded her of Karla's dogged obstinacy. If stubbornness was part of the national character, making Alena Sokol speak might prove to be an uphill struggle.

Not counting Nigel, who had dozed off, none of the others including Miranda Green, with her twenty-odd years of practice, had ever had someone be sick in a session. Reluctant to speak—yes. But puking—no.

Perhaps your client carries inside her something she cannot digest, suggested Juliet Pinchfield. A secret childhood trauma.

They got into a discussion about psychosomatic symptoms and how they manifest inner conflicts. Miranda mentioned several of Freud's women patients who suffered from vomiting and tickling in their throats. This, according to the old master, was due to their fantasies of "sucking at the male organ".

"The old goat," Karla muttered with a disapproving swish of her ponytail, before turning her attention back to Gail. "You seemed surprised that Alena calls Thomas Tomashee. What surprised you exactly?"

It was an innocent enough enquiry but Gail braced herself. And sure enough, Karla followed with, "Because, frankly, in this country people are ignorant about declensions. Which is exactly what Tomashee is—a vocative of Tomash: Tomash, Tomashe, Tomashovie, Tomashe, Tomashee, Tomashovie, Tomashem."

For a moment everyone became pensive. The resulting hush roused Nigel. "Still on goat's organs, are we?" As Miranda's eyes checked each in turn they kept a straight face; in their training it wasn't just the papers you handed in, it was the entirety of you that was being assessed. But there was more to impart: Alena was a Czech version of the name Alice, Karla briefed them. And Sokol actually meant *falcon* in Czech, though the proper female ending would be "ova". By chopping it off Alena had bastardised her name for English ears; her proper name would be Alena Sokolova.

Alice Falcon, Alena Sokolova, rang in Gail's head as she drove back, becoming a particle in a river of cars. What would Alena say if she knew she became a talking point for people she had never met? This, after Gail had assured her that everything was confidential. She felt guilty for disclosing Alena's name; they had all agreed to absolute discretion but what if Alena and Karla had Czech acquaintances in common?

Nearing the Rotherhithe Tunnel Gail joined a queue. They were fed into the tunnel as though into a giant mouth, then propelled forward through the white-tiled gut, the walls splashed by abattoir red from the cars' rear lights, every inch above them weighed by tons of water. On the pavement a lone figure was making his way through this hellish underworld. It was the first time Gail had noticed the tunnel was open to pedestrians. And yet she drove through here sometimes three times a week, there and back like a yo-yo. Tonight, the vehicle behind, with one front light missing, kept dangerously close. Unnerved, Gail accelerated, swerved, and nearly hit an oncoming car. She wanted to shout, make a sound. But her jaw turned sluggish and in her mouth her tongue lay still as a pebble. From then on, the car stayed on her tail, one of its eyes frozen in a malevolent wink. Only after losing it as she turned into her road did her foot on the accelerator relax. But her fingers refused to unlock; she had to pry them open one by one.

No sooner do you come close to someone's mental symptoms than you discover them in yourself, they'd been warned. And indeed, already she couldn't shake off the thought, however absurd, that the car had something to do with Alena Sokolova alias Alice Falcon. As if she had already caught her patient's paranoia.

SIX

On the kitchen table lay a neatly calligraphed note. *Staying in Vauxhall. Deadline. PTO.* On the other side Eddie had written that the telephone engineer had been, did his repairs, and said he had never seen a relay box so *thoroughly burned*. To cause such damage the house must have been hit by lightning: the lightning storm that had hurled Alena Sokol outside Gail's front door.

Mercifully Ben came home not too late. Tomorrow morning, Gail warned him, her patient was due at eight so he must be out by quarter to, at the latest. As this made no visible impression on him, next morning at the stroke of seven she disentangled him from his covers, dragged him into the bathroom, afterwards pressed two croissants into his hand, dropped an apple into his pocket, and pushed him out.

When at eight on the dot Alena Sokol and Thomas materialised on her doorstep and she heard Thomas say, "Not to worry Miss May, I'm only an escort," she felt a rush of joy. Her patient had come back to her! Today Alena's right arm was in a sling fashioned from a dark green scarf patterned with what at first looked like polka dots, but turned out to be rosebuds pink and tight as babies' fists. Her coat, hardly reaching her plump knees, was fixed with a belt that seemed to originate from a different garment. Whether in her mid-thirties or older, even in the harsh brightness of the morning her full smooth cheeks could pass her for an adolescent.

They kept to their sitting arrangements, Alena scanning the room, making sure nothing had changed during her absence. Having scrutinised every corner including the space under the couch, in fairness a moderate response from someone living in fear of being watched, she rested her eyes on Gail. Was she expecting Gail to perform the therapy all by herself? At least now Gail knew that there was no war where Alena came from. But everything about her signalled difference: her manner, her silence, even her smell. In her head swirled foreign thoughts. And not that many miles from Alena's home, where countryside and houses most likely resembled what she knew, people thought nothing of cutting their childhood friends' throats.

Gail let some minutes pass then short-circuited the wait. "How is your arm? Does it still hurt?" In the absence of a response she followed with, "Here you can talk about anything that comes to your mind. Anything you want." She spoke in a casual, light voice. Last night she had read a paper about silence and all the many qualities it could convey. One option was to sit the silence out. The other to voice aloud what it feels like to be with a silent patient, to use your *countertransference*. This was the one she opted for.

"Right now I feel rather tense," she slotted in the space between them. The minuscule shift in Alena's shoulders didn't give anything away. "A bit nervous. Maybe because you're looking at me," Gail added. "Maybe a little worried. Yes. A little apprehensive." She paused to give Alena Sokol a chance. While waiting she ferreted inside herself for the next thing. "Perhaps you feel something similar. But of course you might be thinking something totally different." Then, a moment later, "A bit more relaxed now. And you, Alena?"

38

While serving these platitudes, her heart thumped inside her so loud she worried Alena might hear it. Whatever she said felt inept. Like a deep-sea diver shining a torch she searched within her for a more fertile stratum to offer to Alena. Time ticked on, air floated around them, whether moved by sound or not; speaking or not speaking made no difference. Gradually Alena sank into the armchair, her feet collapsing at her ankles, her thighs falling apart under her skirt. Her eyelids grew heavy. Once she parted her lips, but only to yawn. *Like a baby*, Gail said to herself. *A baby lulled to sleep by mother's voice. And her silence.*

She recalled replicating Ben's sounds when he was an infant; his sounds, his gestures. Famously, Winnicott called this mirroring. Perhaps this was what she needs to be: a mirror reflecting back to Alena her own self. But if this wordless rapport went on indefinitely where would she find the fifteen thousand words for her case study?

When she escorted Alena to the door Thomas was already there, visibly pleased to have her back. "How did my Alenka do today? Any homework for next time?"

"I'm afraid," Gail said, risking being rude, "but this is Alena's therapy. I cannot discuss her with anyone." Thomas said nothing but kept his grin, his features acquiring the look of a noble hound, unfairly kicked.

From the corner by the window she watched them get into their white van. It had a raised roof that could accommodate a wheelchair. Who was the invalid? Her gaze followed their car up the road. Then she noticed them: the Nomads. The tall redhead striding in no-nonsense fashion behind a buggy, a flock of frizzy-haired children of varying ages scampering around. Tagging a few steps behind, arms heavy with supermarket bags was a squat black man, their dad. She had watched them for years: the mother at the helm, the most recent arrival in the pram, the man lugging the ever-bulkier provisions, any time of the day or night. As if their unbridled fecundity condemned them to perpetual motion. Did they have anywhere to rest? Had those kids ever gone to school, their dad to work? There were other regulars she had noticed over the years: the old boy clad from head to toe in identical colour; the ageing lady with a runaway lipstick, pulled by an invisible dog on a non-existent leash; the gaunt gentleman advancing in awkward leaps. Folk you get used to until, having not bumped into them in weeks, you wonder if somewhere not too far-off a smell and a black cloud of flies swarm around a locked door.

Friday being one of Eddie's teaching days they usually had lunch together in the staff canteen. Today, because of his deadline, Gail ate alone, a textbook open by her plate. It was all beginning to make sense: she needed to think of Alena as an infant full of *early libidinal* feelings and no words yet to vocalise them. The thing to do was to let Alena know that she understood her non-verbal communication as a plea. A plea to be loved.

Once she got home she wrote her notes till late. What was the point of going to bed only to be there by yourself? While she undressed she thought of Eddie. She wanted to tell him that she missed him. She let the phone ring but there was no answer. At this hour where would he be? Wasn't the purpose of him staying away to concentrate on his work? She gave it five more minutes before she called again. This time Eddie picked up. They spoke only briefly and, afraid he'd think her childish, she didn't mention anything about missing him. Before going to bed she went downstairs to make sure the door wasn't locked and the outside light was on. She didn't want Ben to have to fumble for keys in the dark. How negligent of her to bear one child only and always have to worry so.

She was woken by footsteps on the stairs. The clock showed 3.13; for the first time ever she had fallen asleep before Ben got home. Behind the door she heard voices whispering, giggling. Ben must have brought a friend—probably Jimmy Rollo who lived further out and sometimes ended up crashing on Ben's floor. In any case, all was well. Her son was back.

A muffled groan disturbed her next. Now the clock's digits said ten past four. Thinking she had dreamed the sound she turned on her side when, from behind the wall, she heard a soft moan. It didn't sound like Ben. Or like Jimmy. There followed a duet of rapid exhalations until, finally, they reached frantic unison. And all along something hard rapped against the floor. The last cry she instinctively knew came from her son. All this was so sudden, so unexpected. As was her response: she was transported to her parents' bed, their dead parents' matrimonial bed, her body stiffened against the agitations next to her: Gillian, having it off with one of the boys, one of the crowd that took to hanging around their parentless house. She hid her head under the cover and sobbed.

In the morning she opened her eyes to the screeching of birds as if she had woken up in the crown of a tree. From her pillow she could see a vast green sea of rippling treetops: a view totally unlike what she had been used to. A few branches jutting out at the very top resembled a figure: a head, a leg, a waving arm, a bough man dancing in the wind. How long before the new growth will make him blend in, disappear? One year? Two? But who knows what happens to branches and leaves; she might be seeing him for years. She flung her arms wide, as if to wave back. Then she remembered the lovers next door.

In the bathroom she instantly knew that her son was the last one to use the toilet. This despite her educational efforts. On the kitchen table she found two glasses, each with a residue of milk. And a half-eaten slice of toast spread with Marmite. The imprint of teeth didn't supply any further clues. Upstairs nothing stirred. On the morning news, Bosnian refugees

41

waiting in the UK for their relatives to be allowed in accused the Home Office of dragging their feet. Accepting only spouses and children under eighteen did seem too rigid. *Children under eighteen.* Absurdly, she felt relieved. Were she and Ben to be torn apart, being only seventeen Ben would be allowed to join her wherever she was. By international agreements he was still classified as a child. A child, for heavens' sake! What have the international agreements to say about children having sex?

SEVEN

"I'm upset," she said, dropping on the couch. "No. I'm angry."

"Tell me," said Horobin.

Gail raised herself on her elbow to peer back at her. "Ben brought home a girl to stay the night. I've no idea who she is."

"Ehum." Was this all Horobin had to say on the subject?

"The wall is so thin I heard everything. Every squeak. Like I was right in that bed with them," she explained, in case Horobin was too ancient to be familiar with the ways of today's youth. "I felt so ..." her voice broke off.

"You *are* upset." From behind her, Horobin placed the tissues beside her head.

"Pissed off, more like. Ben's only seventeen for God's sake!" Usually she didn't use this sort of language with Mrs. Horobin. "Always out, never says a word. And now he has sex with someone I haven't even met, practically next to me! As if he already ... as if I've already—"

"Already lost Ben?" Horobin suggested.

"I'm making your pillow wet," she said, feeling her tears trickle to the back of her neck.

"So that's what's troubling you, Gail May."

So that's what's troubling you, Gail May. Lately the way Phyllis spoke irritated her.

"You fear losing your Benny to a girl?"

"Ben," she corrected Horobin. "Benny was someone else." She did tell Phyllis Horobin how she had lost her parents. But losing Benny, she never got round to telling her. She didn't want Horobin to think of her as someone guaranteed to lose everyone. Everyone she had ever had.

She had met Benny at Manchester University. Tall and lanky, vibrating with energy. Philosophy was his subject. He claimed to carry in his veins Armenian blood. Or perhaps Jewish. The charm of Benny's stories was that they were never fixed. He laughed in squeals and loved it when she washed his hair.

"There was something about Benny, something basic that he must have lacked, you know. Earlier on, in his childhood," she said to Phyllis.

"So you took it on yourself to redress the balance."

And she had. She had cut Benny's toenails, squeezed out the zits on his skinny back, rolled his joints, even pulled on his condoms. One day she felt her nail catching the rubber but thought nothing of it. Or perhaps not quite *nothing*. When, some weeks later, her period failed to arrive, she wasn't surprised. But she'd read enough novels to know not to tell. Benny was headed for great things, the shape of which was yet to come. She was wrong. When she finally told him about her growing cargo Benny was ecstatic. Now they were both anchored. By graduation time her gown hid a sizeable bump. Degrees rolled up in their rucksacks, they headed for London where they rented a room near Finchley Road Tube station. They never thought of looking for jobs. Gail's share from her parents' house was to see them through; they didn't even bother to sign on. They lived on minced beef and spaghetti, the sum total of their cooking expertise. At night they lay on their mattress yin-yang fashion. When the time came

44

for the baby to abseil from her depths it was a shared effort: a triathlon of swimming, crawling, and pushing, with Benny, the father-in-making, massaging her back, timing her breaths, getting under everyone's feet. On hearing his son's first cry he collapsed in a faint on the green hospital lino.

"No one, not even I made much of it then. We assumed he was just too excited."

"Ehum," said Horobin.

Back to their Finchley mattress: now nestled between them their son, their miracle baby with mouth open in perpetual ecstasy, his tiny back coated with soft black down. Except for an occasional bicycle ride to stock up on mince and dry pasta they rarely left their lair. Cocooned in their second-floor haven, their life stretched in front of them seemingly endless. Then one morning, while Gail and their baby son slept, Benny skipped downstairs and unlocked his bike.

"I'd like to think he kissed us before he went," she told Phyllis Horobin.

"I'm sure he did," said Horobin.

When Gail woke up she found Benny's pillow empty. She breastfed Ben, then changed his nappy. She was hungry but except for a lump of cheddar there was nothing in the fridge. The next time she opened her eyes was when the doorbell rang. Coming! she yelled. Benny must've forgotten his keys. What was new? She opened the door to two policemen holding Benny's bicycle between them.

"At first I didn't understand," she said to Horobin. "What serious accident?"

The bike looked just the same—right handlebar slightly bent from when they fell off it together after a party. Behind the cops stood a woman in a tweed coat. I saw it happen, the woman said. She saw the young man turning the corner; saw the truck clipping his shoulder, him flying over the handlebars; the mammoth truck's wheels grating to a halt only inches from him. Passers-by surrounded Benny. He looked Egyptian, the woman said: arms folded at wrong angles, all wrong. Someone slipped a jacket under his cheek while someone else ran to the nearest phone. Benny was unconscious but there was no visible harm. When the ambulance arrived they ripped open Benny's T-shirt to try to restart his heart. The tweed woman was ever so sorry to tell Gail, ever so sorry. The last thing she saw was the truck driver being lifted from his seat. It took two men to carry him down from his cabin.

"What a terrible thing," sighed Horobin. "What a tragedy. It must've been awfully hard for you to manage. And with a baby all by yourself."

After Gail left Horobin she sat in the car, her limbs numb like the wretched truck driver's who believed he had killed Benny. But the autopsy revealed that in Benny's brain a vein had ruptured seconds before the fall. An aneurism, the defect Benny had been born with, that no one knew about. Gail waited for her legs to come to life. She was angry with herself for telling Horobin. Benny wasn't around anymore, but a girl had sneaked into their son's bed. A young cuckoo. She should have gone in and thrown that slut out. A shocking, ugly thought and it was she who thought it. When had she become one of those monster mothers, that's what old Horobin should have made her tackle. Perhaps the time had come to look for someone else. Someone not of Horobin's age, the age you begin worrying about your parents leaving the gas on. If you're lucky enough to still have them.

As she sat there, she saw a man stepping out of the red battered Volkswagen parked in front of her. She had noticed him before slumped in the driver's seat, reading a paper. Now she watched him cross the road and march straight through Horobin's garden gate. The first time she had seen someone else approach Horobin's door. *Her* door that had always magically opened for her. The man brushed his shoulders as if to rid them of dandruff, then rang the bell. And was instantly let in. She checked the time: nine o'clock. The man, whose features she had barely glimpsed but whose brown suit she found positively off-putting, was now about to rest his thinning scalp on the pillow still wet from her tears. Settle his brown acrylic back into the imprint left by her. It was obscene.

She got out of the car. On the back seat of the red Volkswagen she spotted a torn KFC box, on the floor some scattered chips. There was a low wall fronting someone's garden, a part of it collapsed. She lifted a brick, felt its roughness, aimed it at the car's side window. Then carefully inserted it back in its place.

EIGHT

The rains had stopped but it had grown cooler. Winter was definitely on its way. At night a skin of frost turned puddles into black mirrors. They switched the central heating on. Neither she nor Eddie had yet had the honour of being introduced to the person who sometimes took residence in Ben's room and whose sighs they had no choice but get accustomed to; the young pair's couplings an unwelcome reminder of the fluctuating frequency of their own lovemaking. But to forbid Ben bringing his girlfriend in might only make them spend the nights somewhere else. "Thanks mum," was the most she could expect for handing Ben two dinner plates that he hauled straight back to his room. He and Kiko Wunderbar, for that was the name Ben had divulged to them, often got in after she and Eddie had gone to bed. What sort of a mother called her daughter Kiko? And allowed her to stay out overnight? Gail pictured Kiko as a scrawny blonde, the likes of which she noticed hanging around Dulwich and Norwood pubs in their messy school uniforms. At weekends she pictured her in a tight minitop under a chunky bomber jacket, sucking on beer cans, blowing gum: a liability to Ben.

Gail bought a packet of Durex and left it on the bathroom shelf. A day later she found it gone and in its place a note: *Thanks mum. Next time please get Mates.* Outraged, she complied with her son's wish. Their unpredictability alarmed her. What if one day they should bump into her patient?

With Phyllis Horobin, she carried on pretending she had her for herself. After each session, she drove straight off not looking left or right. If the red Volkswagen was lurking somewhere nearby, she did not have to see it. Were she to spot that man again, she wouldn't come back. Also, she had asked Horobin if from now on she could sit in the chair.

"For what reason?"

"Just want to see your face."

"Once or twice we can make an exception," Mrs. Horobin said. "But otherwise, I'm afraid I work only with the couch."

Gail tried to make the most of the time she was given: she watched Phyllis's earlobes tremble with movements of her head; her old bosom heave inside the green cardigan; her swollen legs, the two blood puddings stuffed into thick beige stockings, propped on the stool. On the shelf above her she watched the cacti colony surviving in the permanent chiaroscuro. "Tell me, Gail May, have I done something to lose your trust?" Phyllis had once asked her. She said no.

As for Alena Sokol, the sole change was that these days she came without the sling, sometimes with the rosebuds scarf draped around her neck; probably one of the few items still in her possession from her young days back home. Thomas now kept his distance: he waited for Alena in the van. To make her feel safe, Gail kept the venetian blind permanently drawn. First Alena would subject the room to a detailed scrutiny. Then she would let herself sink into the chair and, her silence as obdurate as ever, pin her gaze on Gail, as if expecting her to read her mind.

"You're looking for something in my face, in my expression, aren't you?" Gail suggested, though she felt on somewhat shaky ground. Alena sighed and dragged her eyes away. This

49

was the moment to put the mirroring theory to the test. "I think you need to see yourself Alena—something about who *you* are reflected in me." Alena Sokol blinked. "Perhaps you need to see me looking at you with … well, with love." Startled, Alena stiffened in her chair. Gail had looked up *love* in the *Dictionary of Psychodynamic Psychotherapy* but of course found nothing there; *love*, it seemed, was impossible to classify. Having started, she carried on: "Yes, love. Like when a mother looks at her baby while feeding it from her breast. The therapist mother looking at baby Alena." Alena Sokol's throat showed a faint tremor, her eyes shot towards the door, and she made as if to rise. "I'm speaking metaphorically, of course," Gail hastily reassured her.

Did her patient think she had lost her mind? At least no one else was there to witness the proceedings. The more mute Alena got, from one silence to the next if this were possible, the more Gail adhered to her strategy. This was how it had to be: whatever there was to know about Alena it had to come from her, from her own free will. On bad days Gail thought of Alena's speechlessness as mere obstinacy. At other times she attributed it to a lack of practice—at home Alena and Thomas probably spoke only Czech. And in her job Alena might be working in a storeroom by herself.

"I believe we have reached an impasse," Gail suggested one day.

"In-pass?"

"When you get stuck."

Though she had nothing to go on but Karla Urbanova's conjecture, in the college library Gail searched for something about the Czech Republic. She found a book published during the communist era, the tone uncompromisingly upbeat: there were photographs of thriving industries, of rippling fields, of women decked out in starched folk costumes, lacy wings protruding from their heads. Gail couldn't picture Alena Sokol wearing one of these. Yet she scrutinised each photo as if she could chance upon her among the jolly dancers. She looked for her in the bare urban squares, under baroque portals. She inspected the windows of apartment blocks. Like a diviner eager for the rod to twitch, Gail hoped her eyes would be drawn to a spot which Alena had once occupied, leaving behind some sort of mirage of herself. When in one photo she spotted, among a group of children, an outline of a pudgy girl, she went to get a magnifying glass. Would she find a lopsided fringe? But under the lens the image broke into incoherent dots.

Before each of their encounters she felt a mounting dread. If the mysterious mechanism by which Alena deposited in her the feelings she couldn't bear in herself was in progress, how was Gail to tell apart Alena's dread and her own?

At supervision Rudi listened, nodded, smacked his lips, scrawled notes in his columns, muttered his *ochos*. Some weeks in he suggested a change of tactic. "If Sou-kol not relating here and now, go in Sou-kol's past."

"How?"

"Ask about her mama and papa."

Gail was astounded. "But aren't you supposed to wait for what the client brings? You're not supposed to impose your own agenda."

"Gail!" Rudi's arms shot up. "Therapy not about theory, therapy about *relationships*. Sometimes forgetting theory *number one!*"

Next time, after Alena had checked everything in the room, as per usual, Gail straightened in her chair. "I'd like to ask you something, Alena." She spoke loud and clear. "Since we're still new to each other perhaps you could tell me about your background." Like a bird listening to another's trill Alena tilted her honey-coloured bob. "Your parents, your siblings ..." Gail explained: "Your mother and father."

For a moment Alena Sokol's head remained at its angle. Thinking over her proposition? Then she drew a breath and

51

spoke. This was so unexpected that later Gail couldn't separate what Alena had said from what she herself had inferred. It was as if each sound, each half-begun word, was an invitation to complete it herself. As if everything in the room gained contours and even the air became sharper. And all it took was a simple question.

Alena Sokol was indeed Czech. Czech from Czechoslovakia. She had come to England from her father—from her father in Prague ... They had lived on a main road ... In Prague every tram stop had a name, the one near their block of flats was called *By the Bell*. Another one *By the Tank, By the Angel* and so on ... Tata called Alena his "pigeon", his *"ho-lub"*. He would sniff her hair and go—*hmm, best pigeon perfume* ... *Tata*, Gail guessed, meant "father". But Alena's mother, where was she? During Alena's *birthday*, she had died. So that was it: Alena's mother died while giving birth to Alena, the trauma that had left her patient speechless—the trauma that had struck far, far back in Alena's infancy. Then there was an electrical engineer from Slovakia. Or was it Slovenia, Gail didn't catch which. Who was Nicola? Tata's name—Nicola. Tata Nicola did everything for Alena, even taught her how to use a camera ... how light illuminated silver crystals ... The bottles of chemicals in the bathroom smelled of what Alena called *kee-ke-la-ku-ka*. Watching Alena's face, saliva instantly flooding her mouth, Gail knew what kee-ke-la-ku-ka meant: a pickle. Tata Nicola showed his daughter how to agitate the photos in their tray. And Gail saw Alena watching, spellbound, the floating pictures coming to life. She saw Alena's father passing her the slimy papers, saw Alena's bare legs balancing on a stool as she stretched to hang the wet photos on the washing line. In the glow of a single red bulb Gail felt their closeness: Tata and Alena. And if Gail's imaginings had something to do with her own yearning for her father, so be it. From where else were you to know these things if not from yourself?

52

Near the end of the session Alena Sokol suddenly dangled in front of Gail a black-and-white photo. At first Gail registered no more than a blur of textures. Gradually she made out a sky ... a stretch of water. Then a tiny spot, a pinprick between the waves: a buoy, a bird? Someone's head? Hard to tell, the photo was buckled and stained. She would have liked to look closer but Alena had slipped the photo back into her purse.

Gail had already let the time overrun by three minutes, and keeping time was the principal tenet of psychotherapy. "Time's up," she said and followed Alena to the door. Then, releasing her into the evening dusk, her curiosity got the better of her. "On that photo, Alena, who was it in the water? Was it your father?"

What made her say this she couldn't tell, she just did. Of course by now the therapy was over. When the hour is over you're not to talk to your patient, not under any circumstances. Talking to your patient outside the session breaches one of the most basic rules; such a blunder could easily jeopardise your qualification. Yet, having once trespassed the sacred boundary, what was the point of holding back now? "Your father," Gail kept on while Alena Sokol gaped at her wide-eyed, "Where is he? Also in England?"

"Con," said Alena in a voice so quiet that Gail wasn't sure what she meant. Con or gone? About to ask again, in the corner of her eye she spotted a pair of trousered legs hurrying towards them.

"I see you've already fallen under Alenka's spell!"

Aware that Thomas had witnessed her transgression, her misconduct, Gail quickly retreated back.

Her notes covered several pages. At first she had been starved of any facts and now she had almost too many to make sense of. To clear her thoughts she threw on her coat and went out. The streets were empty: not even a sign of the Nomads. In most windows a bluish light flickered, as if an alien form had mutated from house to house. At the end of the street, where the park began, at even intervals lamps dotted the path, like a scaled-down runway. Ideas raced through her head: what exactly did Alena mean when she called her father a *con*? That he was a fraudster of some kind, a conjurer of images? The other possibility was that Alena Sokol's father was not a *con* but was *gone*. Gone where?

NINE

While undressing she caught sight of herself in the mirror: arms lightly freckled, breasts a little on the ripe side but still firm, auburn hair not entirely natural but near enough. All in all, it wasn't too bad. Pulling on her nightie she watched her breasts ride high and wished Eddie would look up. And he did. Briefly. Then, smiling, he went back to his magazine. Peeling off your clothes to arouse a man, running your knickers between your thighs, did women do this only in strip clubs? She got into bed, settled next to Eddie, caressed his ear. Like with everything on Eddie she found nothing superfluous there, not even a protruding earlobe. She wished him to desire her. Also, she wished she could tell him about her breakthrough with Alena: how she had been raised by her father whom Gail envisaged as a charming but fickle character. And how, even before hearing about it, she had felt that something had gone terribly wrong in Alena's early life.

"Eddie?" She pressed her face into his shoulder. Eddie kept his eyes on his page, though in his profile she caught a slight shift. "You know that patient I have?" Still unwilling to interrupt his reading, Eddie nodded. "Well, I guessed her silence was caused by her traumatic beginnings."

"Oh. Really?"

"Yes. And we've made progress. She has now moved from non-verbal dyad into the stage of language. Dyad means mother and infant," she added for clarity.

"Isn't she an adult already?" Eddie peered at her over his glasses. Then with the top of his hand he tested her cheek. "You should take it easy."

Whenever she had attempted to tell Eddie something about her work he would let her know that he found it in slightly bad taste. Perhaps he was right—prattling on about her patient, getting short of breath, it was unprofessional of her. She watched him reading, the light picking out gold in his moustache. One of these days she would ask him to give up his flat, move in with her, and rent a studio for work. Surely by now the two of them had outgrown the old arrangement. After a while Eddie ceremoniously took off his reading glasses and drew her to him. As they kissed she heard the front door. For a moment she considered accosting the young couple by the fridge. But they must have come home with full stomachs because already she heard them stomping up the stairs. Tomorrow, she promised herself, feeling Eddie's hand on her thighs, tomorrow I'll demand to meet that girl. On hearing the door to Ben's room bang her legs locked together, as if by reflex.

"You've got the visitors?"

"We have," she whispered, ignoring Eddie's silly euphemism. "They might hear us."

"So? We hear them."

"It could traumatise Ben. You know. The primal scene."

"The primal scene?" Eddie groaned. "I'm not even his dad."

Every time Eddie denied his tie to her son, it hurt her. "I'm talking symbolically," she said, feeling her nipples harden against Eddie's chest, in spite of herself.

"I'm not." He guided her hand to his penis.

Why did he always have to let her know he wasn't Ben's dad? This, after he had been around for most of Ben's life. She should ask him about it. But with his hand coaxing her head down, the timing didn't seem right. She couldn't remember whose idea it was that before taking his cock in her mouth she would feel his balls with her tongue. Still, she liked their lemony scent, their texture reminding her of the translucent jellied sweets they once ate in a Chinese restaurant.

She opened the bathroom door to the hum of an electric toothbrush and the sight of a slender, dusky arm.

"Hi Gail, I'm Kiko. I'm nearly done." The arm belonged to a tall lanky girl in an orange sleeveless top with *Scooby-Doo* printed over two tiny mounds. Large freckles over a wide nose, crinkly hair bunched in two stumps, one tied with a fluorescent green rubber band, the other with a blue one. "You're running low on toothpaste." Kiko Wunderbar calmly slipped the electric toothbrush identifiable by its blue band as belonging to Eddie back in its stand—Eddie whose meticulousness about hygiene Gail had learned to respect. "If you want," Kiko offered, "I'll get some tomorrow."

Back in bed Gail tried to discern the silence next door. Had there been a whispered exchange of words, an argument? Having come face to face with Kiko Wunderbar, the outrage she had felt before was now replaced by concern. Ben was perfectly capable of holding it against Kiko that she had engaged in a "conversation" with his mother—there could be a standoff, they could be lying with their backs to each other—hers light caramel, his white. And she—the cause of their agony. She considered getting up and knocking on their door under some pretext when she heard a burst of laughter. All was well. Beside her Eddie breathed regularly, blowing small bubbles on the out-take. She lifted his arm and wrapped it around her like a heavy luxurious shawl. In his sleep Eddie smiled. In the crook of his elbow she sniffed his intricate aroma. Her breasts were cool where she had washed off his offering, albeit spent in the wrong place. But she was forty-one; her time had most likely passed. She counted her riches: with Eddie by her side and the two young lovers next door, her head swirling with ideas about her patient, her life was full, the fullest yet. And even that mean little creature crouched inside her, the voice who whispered that no good will ever come to her, she was on her way to conquer. In the window the sky began to lighten. Perhaps this was happiness.

"Morning! You're not making these for us, are you?" Emerging from her son's bedroom Kiko Wunderbar sauntered into the kitchen on her giraffe limbs.

How old was she? Not underage, Gail hoped. She carried on buttering the bread. "I have a patient coming at eight. So you and Ben need to hurry up. You must be out by ten to."

"Excuse me." Kiko's elegant fingers prised the knife from her. "My mum never makes my sandwiches! Or for my sis. No way. And Afua's only thirteen." She pushed the salad leaves and the packet of ham aside and from the depth of the cupboard produced a jar of Nutella. She smeared each slice with a generous layer, then expertly chopped two bananas and plonked the slices on as if paving a road. From close by, Gail could see that her freckles were interspersed with tiny bumps, like sprinklings of fine semolina.

Kids, they're still kids. And that mum who refuses to make sandwiches, was she white or black? "What do your parents do, Kiko?"

"One's a midwife, the other a doctor." Kiko delved in the drawer and rolled out a generous length of silver foil. Probably a white doctor falling for a black nurse, Gail thought. As if she could hear her, Kiko shot her a glance. "Mum's doctor and dad's midwife." She relished the moment. "Mum's from Ghana and dad's Dutch."

"I see." Gail busied herself with something or other. "Is Kiko a Ghanaian name then?"

"Mum! Kiko's Ja-pa-nese!" Ben had materialised in the door. "There was a famous hurricane named Kiko, haven't you

58

heard?" He put his arm around his girlfriend's waist. "Her surname means *excellent* in German."

First time she'd seen them next to one another: Ben a good inch and a half shorter than Kiko.

"Yep." Kiko punched the air. "Excellent hurricane—c'est moi! Mind you, 'gale in May' is also wicked. But Ben May? I don't think so." Kiko comically wrinkled her nose; her skin had the soft firmness of best-quality fudge. "Is only us cool people that have funky names." She dropped the sandwiches into their rucksacks, tossed an apple in each, aimed her leg at Ben's bum. "Come on Bensy! We're outa here." Smiling, her son kicked her back.

TEN

The next two sittings yielded a plethora of details: about how Alena had arranged to come from Prague to England to work in a Butlins holiday camp and all that had followed. Gail scribbled her notes at a feverish pitch. She couldn't wait to bring it all to supervision. Sure enough, as soon as she started, Rudi rubbed his knees. "I told you, Gail. It was a question of time."

First she sketched out Alena Sokol's origins, her father's origins, and of course Alena's mother's untimely death. Telling Rudi about it Gail noticed his eyes flutter and felt proud. To have made Alena's loss alive to him seemed like an achievement.

"Poor Sou-kol," Rudi said, "starting life with maternal deprivation. That's why she acts like a dead mother to you, not speaking. Making you feel like an abandoned child. A child begging for love."

"Alena being a dead mother to me and I an abandoned child to her?" Not in a million years could she have come up with something like this by herself.

"Yes! To you—dead. Unapproachable. Is important to Sou-kol that you experience the same she felt. *Transference/countertransference*—is all there. Bravo!" Rudi's small palms patted each other.

To suggest that this was what went on between her and Alena felt mad. And at the same time shockingly right. Without being there Rudi Chang knew. Now he patiently waited for her to note it all down. "So you saying Sou-kol came from Czechoslovakia straight to Butlins? Ocho! Abroad first time and by herself! Sou-kol's adventurous, isn't it?"

"Yes, wasn't she?" She felt as if her own child had been praised. "I think the requirement was to be over eighteen. And fluent in English. But the only English words Alena knew were *thank you* and *yesterday*."

"*Yesterday*?"

"Because of the Beatles, I assume." Hearing Rudi sigh to himself *you assume?* she quickly added, "She did mention the Beatles, I'm pretty sure."

"OK. OK. So when Sou-kol arrived?"

She looked in her notes. "In 1968. She was barely sixteen. In fact, that makes us the same age."

When Gail was fifteen, with their father gone, it was now their mother's turn to leave them, little by little, day by day. One afternoon when Gillie happened to be out, Gail heard her rasp for breath. Then again and again, as if a mechanism was grinding to a halt. By the time Gillie got back, everything was over.

"1968. Prague Spring, what was his name?" Rudi Chang rubbed his forehead. "Dubcek! Happened the same year Hisamata Shinchi travelled to Switzerland to meet Carl Gustav Jung."

The name of the Czech leader sounded familiar. Who Carl Gustav Jung was she knew, though he didn't feature on their reading list, their leaning being Freudian and Kleinian. The other name she had never heard.

"Beg you pardon!" Rudi flapped his arms. "1958, not '68 Hisamata Shinchi went to Switzerland. So, how can psychoanalysis finish suffering, the Buddhist master asked the other. And Carl Gustav Jung? He says: to liberate yourself from

61

collective unconscious you need to be an individual. Ocho! But what do you know?" Rudi Chang clicked his tongue. "Zen doesn't believe in the individual, Zen believes in—" A series of howls resonated through the house. Rudi stuck his pen behind his ear. "Is my boy, excuse me, Gail."

While he was gone she tried his couch to get a taste of how it would feel to be Rudi Chang's patient. The rug was coated in a blanket of fine black hair that settled densely in its folds, like dust. Rudi once told her that every time a patient was due he had to drag Gustav from the room by force. Rudi's patients and supervisees were here on sufferance, the rest of the time it was just the two of them: Gustav stretched on the couch and Rudi in his analytic chair.

On his return Rudi's lips were twitching in a smile. "Please continue, Gail. About Hisamata Shinchi we can chat some other time."

She read on. "When Alena arrived she was shocked. A holiday camp by the sea with barbed-wire fence and searchlights? In Prague Alena saw a Butlins brochure. It showed a palm, which made her imagine she'd be like a barmaid in a Riviera hotel. Like she saw in foreign films."

"Gail, *barmaid in a Riviera hotel*? Did Sou-kol say that?"

"That's what I understood."

Rudi scratched his scalp. Gail had never been to Butlins but Alena's account, however minimal, made her see the rickety chalets where the staff slept, the gaudy old-time ballroom; smell the grimy cloth Alena was given to wipe the plastic tables with; taste the Horlicks at midnight, to the sounds of "God Save the Queen". Of course to Alena all this was a novelty. As she read, Gail registered the busy scrawling of Rudi's pen and out of the corner of her eyes, his smile. She felt like an actor on a stage. "What Alena Sokol loved most," she told Rudi, "was to go to the beach, stretch out on the sand, and listen to the tide. By then the Russian army had massed around

Alena's country's borders. Alena saw the pictures on TV. The situation was serious, her father wrote. Then, out of the blue he arrived with a suitcase."

"Crossing all the borders from Prague?"

"Yes. At night Alena smuggled him in through a hole in the fence."

"Ocho!" Rudi stabbed the paper with his pen. "Nocturnal entry through a hole!"

The sexual connotation seemed a little over the top but she noted it down anyway. "The girl who slept on the lower bunk went to stay with a friend so Alena's father could use her bed. In the middle of the night someone rushed in. Russian tanks had invaded their country! There was shooting in the streets. In a shock Alena and her father waited till first light. Then they went out. The beach was empty, the sea murky—"

"Gail! Gail please stop!" Rudi interrupted her again, his small rounded nostrils flaring. "Invasion, murky sea, shooting ... is television drama! But how is it for you, you Gail to sit there with Sou-kol and listen? What you feel—your *counter-transference*, Gail? Is missing."

How was she to explain to Rudi Chang that monitoring what she felt was the last thing on her mind? That all her time, all her energy went into deciphering a flicker of an eye, a shrug, an odd word here and there. And if she wasn't able to vouchsafe every single detail? Intuitively she knew it all to be true. She saw Alena watching her father wade in the waves, looked with her through the camera viewfinder, one moment catching his head, next seeing it dip in the swell.

"Russians invade the country and papa Sou-kol goes swimming?"

"I've seen the photo. The invasion, it was a national tragedy. But her father had never swum in the sea before, there was no sea where he came from."

"Slovenia has sea," Rudi objected. "The Mediterranean."

She leafed back in her notes. "Did I say he came from Slovenia? I'm sorry, I must have meant Slovakia. Slovakia doesn't have a sea, does it?"

"No. It has blue Danube. Uhm-uhm-uhm-uuuhmm ..." Rudi hummed through his nose the well-known waltz. Then he nodded to her to go on.

"Alena told me she lay on the beach listening to the waves. When she stood up again there was no sign of her father. She knew he was a good swimmer so she didn't worry. Well, not at first."

Rudi pinched his mouth, shook his head.

"She shouted his name and ran into the water. Other people came, their questions too much for what English she had picked up in her two weeks of service."

Poised above the page Rudi clutched his pen, his brows raised in two question marks. "And papa Sou-kol?"

"That was the end of the session."

"I see." Rudi snapped in and out the tip of his pen, put aside his notebook, and massaged his shiny scalp.

ELEVEN

Their last seminar before Christmas. On the gleaming desk, around which they usually probed the theory, lay plastic tubs with refreshments and two bottles of Bull's Blood Miranda Green had brought in her bike basket. Their impromptu banquet at odds with the Victorian splendour of the oak wall panelling, the black marble maidens flanking a massive fireplace nowadays kitted out with gas rings.

The mere fact of Alena Sokol regularly turning up made Gail a full member of this exclusive family. When they had first started there were seven of them. But courses such as theirs expected a high fallout, and their year bore the brunt of it. Today, their patients were strictly off limits, the theme was to be light-hearted, festive.

"Listen!" Nigel was already a little tipsy. "Not that this has anything to do with Christmas. But ever since I was a wee lad, guess what I thought? Guess!" He hiccupped with excitement, the freckles giving his face an orange tint. "I thought ... I thought that *pooing* ... wait for it! I thought that *pooing* is something you grow out of! Yep! Like you grow out of nappies."

"Well, they do say that most psychological disorders start in early childhood," Karla Urbanova interjected.

"No, seriously. I thought, how could grown-ups go on fabricating something so stinky from their bottoms." Nigel glanced around as if still waiting for a definitive answer, his childhood bewilderment still in evidence.

"Interesting," said Miranda, her greying curls loosened from her bun. "As we know, to produce a poo for your parents is a generous offering. A creation that needs to be gratefully received. If not, you might be feeling messy all your life. Of course, it can also affect other things. Like sex for example."

"Why mix evacuation with sex?" Karla asked, crunching on a celery stick. Until now Gail hadn't noticed that Karla's jaw emitted a faint click.

"Why not? It's only the next-door department, isn't it?" Nigel chuckled. "Mind you—a different hole."

"Not necessarily," Juliet Pinchfield blurted out, instantly blushing.

"Whoa!" Nigel gave them all a wink. "Look who's talking!"

And this from Juliet, whose voice you could hear only if you strained your ears. They looked around at each other: anal sex, who was into it? Juliet's blush spread to the roots of her hair. "Actually it can be very confusing," she said, taking a deep breath. "When I was small I thought that if you strained hard down there, you know …"

"Hard stool's always a bit of a bother, Jul." Nigel stood up and slapped one of the fireplace maidens' black marble rump.

"What I thought was that your bottom might fall off," Juliet whispered. "I must've heard it somewhere. Honestly! Something down there falling off, it used to terrify me." The relief of telling them brought on a fit of giggles.

"These childhood preoccupations often suggest all sorts of frightening fantasies: castration anxiety for example …" Miranda suggested with a deadpan face.

"In a girl?" Karla Urbanova enquired.

Nigel hurried to their colleague's aid, blobs of spittle spraying his red V-neck. "You've no willy to speak of, have you Jul?" Bull's Blood had turned Nigel's eyes rat pink. "Don't worry Jul, we're all fuck-ups. Fucked over by our parents."

A silent exchange of looks. The common understanding was that Nigel, a social worker with a troubled personal history, wouldn't last the course. In fact he had already dropped out once, only to reappear after a few weeks.

It was now either Karla's or Gail's turn, as it was highly unlikely that their tutor Miranda would add anything personal to the pot. Dutifully, Gail searched her mind for something from her childhood, something risqué. And sure enough, the white ceiling with its frosty plasterwork brought an unexpected memory that took her by surprise: dunes of snow, so blindingly white that she must keep her eyes scrunched. Gripped between her father's legs she is plummeting down a slope, holding onto a rope; through her glove it cuts into her palm. The wind whooshes in her ears, the trees rush by. Her father's stretched legs do the steering. Where are Mummy and Gillie? On another sledge behind them, probably. Suddenly they hit a tree stump and she lands on her side, slides down on the sharp snow. Darkness flips in her eyes. Next, she is carried in a giant's arms as if she had shrunk into a miniature of herself, not bigger than one of his fingers, head bumping up and down as light as a snowflake. With every giant's step, her left hip seems to grow and the giant's warm breath brings heat inside her legs. She worries that she has wetted herself. In her hip the throbbing pain is now delicious. When her father takes off her clothes to check if anything is broken she is surprised that her tights are dry. A bruise on her left hip, smaller than a coin, is all there is. And only much, much later does she sense this was her first orgasm. An orgasm that, in a shocking equation, ties her to her father.

Gail said she was sorry but from her childhood she couldn't remember a thing. Nothing funny, nothing worth mentioning. Nothing about potty training.

"Well, I for one don't have a problem remembering my *po-tty trai-ning.*" Karla Urbanova sarcastically minced her words. "Actually it was pretty straightforward."

What? they probed, leading her on. What was pretty straightforward? Their ever-present, unspoken sense of rivalry made Gail suddenly fear for Karla.

"Well, once I was in bed, that was it!" Karla laughed. "I just wasn't allowed to use the toilet."

"But what if you absolutely had to?" Juliet asked.

"I didn't. I learned to hold it till the morning."

Persecutory! Sadistic! Karlie, were your parents communists? Nigel paraded his outrage. As for Gail, she wondered if Karla's home regime was typical and if Alena Sokol had been subjected to similar education.

"Personally ... personally I can't see what's so wrong with teaching a child some self-control," Karla said. "What's the point of pathologising everything? Can't we sometimes take things as they are?"

Used to Karla's provocations they looked to their teacher to defend their science. Or was it art?

"I'm afraid we can't take things as they are," Miranda obliged. The gossip was that besides a doctoral degree her credentials included having in her youth slept with a legendary Argentinean psychoanalyst whose own analyst had trained under Freud. "Perhaps what you might have learned was," Miranda turned to Karla, "that there's something about you, something vital you must control and suppress. Otherwise you risk losing your parents' love."

"That so?" An unexpected quiver entered Karla's voice. She pulled a strand of hair and strangled her finger with it till the tip went purple.

"But then, people have always thought of good reasons for not allowing little girls to wander about at night, haven't they?" Miranda checked around them. "Like witnessing parental intercourse."

Karla Urbanova stood up. "I think Miranda what you just said is perverse!" She got into her coat and picked up her two briefcases. "Merry Christmas everyone!" She slammed the door behind her, causing the air freshener to fall from the wall, releasing a whiff of pine forest. They heard the clip-clop of her heels on the stairs. Over the years they each had shared crumbs about their private lives. Except for Karla; all they knew about her was that her partner's name was Chris.

"Well!" Miranda poured around the rest of the wine. "I'm sure each of us has our doubts sometimes, that's inevitable."

"Speaking of which I have something to tell you," peeped Juliet. Just as the very core of their shared belief was questioned, here was Juliet Pinchfield offering to soothe them with her mild ways. What Juliet wanted to share with them was that her training patient had secured for himself a new job.

Excellent, they congratulated her. A patient of hers doing well reflected well on Juliet; Nigel went as far as smacking a wet kiss on her cheek.

"The job's in Germany," Juliet whispered. "I'm afraid I can't see myself starting all over again with someone new."

The very thing they had collectively dreaded. But to give up now, in the penultimate year? What a waste! They made Juliet promise that she would look for someone new. Not solely for her sake, that went without saying, but also to spare their shrinking tribe another cull.

TWELVE

Even when alone, Gail kept to her side of the bed, a statement—if only to herself—of this being but a temporary state of affairs. There were whispers behind the wall, quickened breaths. And then the sound of rhythmical knock-knocking against the floor. In the morning, after they're gone Gail would find the offending leg on Ben's bed and prop it up. Instantly she felt less at the mercy of what went on next door. But when there was a cry not even she—a mother—could tell from whose young throat it tore out. And yet, when Ben was born, she had instantly known his yelling from all the other yellings on the ward. Long after next door drew quiet she was kept awake by a rattling windowpane. One of these days she would find someone to see to it. And to all other windows and to the eucalyptus tree and everything else overgrown in the garden. She might even ask Ben to help her, now that he's old enough to have carefree sex.

She opened a book by a renowned analyst. As she read she found herself falling in love with him, him and his astonishing insight into humans with all their secrets, their inadequacies. She felt he knew about her more than she knew herself and she wished he were her own therapist. In the dark her fingers began trailing the stretches and dips of her: over her breasts to her belly and further, in leisurely increments. She inhaled her own perfume on her fingers and thought of Eddie. She could call him. Put on a voice. A little husky, perhaps. Tell him where her fingers went. Use explicit language. Juliet Pinchfield probably wouldn't think twice about giving something like this a chance, bashful as she was. For all Gail knew most women wouldn't, though she couldn't see Alena enticing Thomas to listen to an exploration of her personal topography. But then Alena mostly managed without words. Gail picked up the phone and dialled Eddie's number. Engaged. She waited then tried again. And then many more times. Nothing unusual for Eddie to work throughout the night. But being on the phone this late was another matter. Again Alena sneaked into her head, in fact hardly a day had gone by that she didn't think of her. Alena alone on that beach, waiting for Tata to resurface from the waves. Of course not comparable to waiting for Eddie to pick up the phone. Yet intolerable all the same.

In the short distance between the front door and the car the wind cut into her. Her legs, squashed in the jeans she had pulled over her nightie, felt stiff and awkward. Peering through the mist she drove at a snail's pace, the condensation so bad she had to keep wiping the windscreen with her sleeve. And yet she saw nothing. Only when she felt a soft thud against the front bumper did she glimpse a mop of fur—like one of those floppy puppets Ben used to watch on Sunday morning children's TV. It shuffled to the curb and disappeared under someone's garden hedge.

It took a moment for Eddie to come to the door. When he finally appeared he wore his blue cotton shirt, the one that always smelled of parched grass. His hair was tousled; under his eyes were shadows of tiredness.

"What're you doing here?"

"I drove and hit ..." She began to sob, more from relief at seeing Eddie than anything else. At first he thought her car had hit a person. "No, no, I think it was a fox. It ran away."

"On its last legs most likely, with mange." Eddie grimaced with disgust. "You probably helped it out of its misery." To be put out of her misery, wasn't this why she had come? She was grateful to feel his arm around her, grateful to be led in.

Eddie had bought his council flat when the right-to-buy scheme came into existence. He knocked two rooms into one and compressed the kitchen into a silver pod you had to access through an oval door as if stepping into a space capsule. Or a chapel where Eddie was the chief priest. In the main room, along the length of the wall Eddie had fixed a desk made from buffed metal sheeting. Here, gliding on his swivel chair equipped with pneumatic castors, Eddie worked.

The bedroom was equally spartan: a cabin with a wall-to-wall berth you had to climb into on all fours and a partly blocked window so that you had only sky to gape into, rather than the shared yard. It was rare for her to spend the night here. From between dark maroon sheets she watched Eddie winding down his computer programs, the spotlights in the ceiling giving everything a bluish tint. She thought of the Danish artist to whose exhibition Eddie once took her and whose name she forgot: paintings of tantalisingly empty rooms occasionally occupied by a sole figure, her back to the viewer. Some doors were left ajar but who had passed through them remained a mystery. Eddie admired the paintings' pervading absence. But she stuck to her own version: not an absence but an invitation, a promise.

When she woke up, at first she didn't know where she was. From the other room she heard Eddie talking in a quiet tone. She glanced at the clock: 6.30; she had slept through the night. When Eddie came in he already wore his corduroy trousers but no shirt.

"Who was it?"

"Oh just someone from college."

Against the wall, the paleness of Eddie's naked torso appeared as radiant as if it had been underpainted by red. Unprompted, here was a memory: a man is being dragged out from a lake. *Doctor! Is there any doctor here?* The call travels along the bank. Her parents run to help and she runs after them. It was the first time she saw a naked man's body; the grey-yellow skin, a dark brush under his long belly that someone quickly covered with a towel, a green trickle from his mouth that instantly made her regret her curiosity: Thanatos and Eros, warring.

She sat up. "Last night, when your phone kept being engaged, I couldn't bear not knowing who you were talking to so late." Now that her face was level with his waist, she looped her arms around his hips. "You don't have to tell me but I just wanted you to know why I came."

Slowly Eddie began to stroke her hair, there and back. She pressed her cheek against the soft ribs of the fabric, felt his excitement. "I don't mind telling you," he said, lowering himself over her, his moustache grazing her neck. "It was the same person who called just now, a new tutor. She is finding it all, you know—too much. For some reason she got it into her head that I'm the one to help her."

"How are you supposed to help her?"

"Search me," he murmured, his face taking on a transfixed, almost tormented look, the look that she knew. That she adored. Across his shoulder she saw his toes dig into the mattress. He arched over her and she held onto him with all her strength.

It wasn't yet eight o'clock when Gail parked the car but the white van was already in its usual place. She glanced up and down the road—no sign of Alena or of Thomas. Hoping that Ben and Kiko had already left she raced up the stairs. She changed in seconds, even managed to slap on some make-up. Around her the house remained hushed, and from outside too all sounds had ceased. As if, while she'd been at Eddie's, some world-shattering event had taken place and they were the last people on earth. The consulting room was dark, the shutters drawn. She bent to pick up from the coffee table the cup and saucer she had left there last night and as she straightened, right there in front of her a dark silhouette slowly rose up. Freezing in mid air, Gail let everything drop. Only when the china hit the carpet did she shriek.

"The door," said Alena Sokol. "It was open."

It must have happened when she had run in: she must have left the door open. Ben and Kiko! While she was in her bedroom what if someone else had sneaked in and found his way into Ben's room? A random criminal, a murderer stumbling upon the unsuspecting lovers? Now she remembered the ominous silence. She must go and investigate. She was about to make an excuse when she heard two pairs of feet prance down the stairs. As they passed she caught her son's unfamiliarly raw voice. "I'm not a fucking robot, you know." Then Kiko hissed something back and they were gone.

She looked at Alena. "I apologise for this."

Unaware that overhearing other people's conversation during your therapy was not the done thing, Alena remarked that *robot* came from *robota*, a Czech word. While talking, she pulled out of her bag a bunch of roughly printed black-and-white photos and thrust them under Gail's nose: a pair of old-fashioned glasses; a half-open address book; a bunch of keys, each labelled with a tag on a string. It took a moment before Gail realised what she was looking at: Alena's father's belongings, the forensic evidence left on the beach after he had plunged into the tide. So there never was a reunion of father and daughter. Poor Alena, having to lose her father in such a way. As if there was some better way of losing one's father.

"Oh, Alena." Gail steadied her voice. Crying in front of your patient, bringing in your own sorrow, wasn't on. "This must've been so very, very hard for you."

In the absence of a reaction Gail carried on flipping through the photos: a puffa jacket, a child's rucksack, a woman's coat with a fur collar, a glass jar filled with dark liquid, a wrist bangle, each with its own label; a tattered pushchair, an umbrella, a handbag, a worker's helmet, a teddy bear … An inventory. That had nothing do with Alena's father and his demise.

Gail had once read that our earliest memories are stored in our brain like unprocessed photographic exposures, waiting there to be developed and printed. But why would Alena take pictures of things that she handled in her job? Things that used to belong to people she had never met. What sense could Gail make of them? A child's buggy—a fertility symbol; an umbrella—a phallic one; a bag—the vagina … Perhaps picture taking was just simply something that Alena Sokol has been programmed for by her Tata.

Outside, the overcast sky turned the day into night. Cars' headlights threw shadows on the wall: silhouettes, branches, abstract patterns … In all this flux one shape, like a distorted, magnified profile from a children's picture book reappeared a few times. Then, just as it became swallowed by the next wave of darkness the doorbell rang. There was a mute exchange of glances between them. Gail checked the time: still twenty minutes to go so it couldn't be Thomas. In their training they had debated this sort of situation when someone comes to read the gas meter or deliver a package. The consensus was you carry on with the session no matter what. It was at moments like these that you demonstrated your commitment to your patient. Several loud knocks followed, echoing through the house. Under her honey fringe Alena's face drained and her hands gripped the armrests, her breath coming in shallow, terse gulps. Was this what hyperventilation looked like? To the best of Gail's knowledge there was not a single paper bag in the house.

"Alena?" Gail leant forward. "What are you afraid of?"

Alena gawped at her with round baby seal's eyes. Those baby seals with no arms to hug each other, only flaps, that everyone was so eager to save from being massacred for their soft pelt. The panic pushed her deeper into the chair. The strain in Gail's own body told her this was more than mere *counter-transference*; this was Alena's terror pouring straight into her. But what if there really was a cause for concern? Maybe she should call the police. To tell them what? That someone had knocked on her front door in the middle of the day?

"Don't worry, I'm not going to open," she said, suddenly noticing that, after years of quiet service, the radiator had developed an unpleasant hiss, like a sick person's protracted breath. "But tell me—do you actually think that … that someone's following you?"

Alena stared at her. "Why you ask?"

"Because of the way you reacted. Just now."

"Tomash said this to you?"

"No, not to me."

"Because Tomash doesn't believe it's true."

From then on there were no more knocks. Whoever it was by the door must have given up.

As Gail hurried to the train that invisible presence kept turning her head, making her inspect every corner, behind every tree. With their faux Greek pillars and "Gothic" stonework the houses seemed an ideal setting for a horror film. It wasn't by chance that only a few corners away Edgar Wallace, the crime novelist, had once lived.

At the station the platform was nearly empty, the regular commuters gone. She sat down and opened her book. According to the theory, patients sometimes try to communicate with the therapist by projecting their terrifying feelings—their unwanted objects—into them, she read. For this, *projective identification* was the right term; it could make the therapist lose her sense of herself as if living in someone else's fantasy. As if under her patient's hypnotic spell.

She boarded the nearly empty train, still reading. Sitting down by the window she registered that a man sat right next to her. In the periphery of her vision she noticed his watch with its old-fashioned fluorescent dial; her father used to wear a similar one. As the train picked up speed she felt her insides reverberate to its whining and grating.

Shortly before London Bridge they came to a halt. Outside, there was an apartment block with a terrace fenced by potted trees, the glass door half open. She made out a sofa, two armchairs, and someone's bare back. Then another train obliterated the view. And then she saw everything once more: the terrace, the glass partition, the plants, but the back was now gone. No matter how many times she will pass by nothing will ever be the same, life is uncatchable. When she looked back, her book had tumbled from her lap to the floor. She reached for it but the hand with the watch got there first.

"*Ob-ject The-ory* ..." the man spelled out part of the title. An impressive face, a sharp profile, a leonine white mane— someone who could impersonate one of those marble Roman busts. "Let me guess," the man passed her the book. "You're a physicist."

"No. A psychotherapist." Her declaration took her by surprise. Jumping ahead of herself, was she? They pulled into the station. When her fellow passenger stood up she experienced a moment of disappointment: a head like this deserved to sit on a taller frame.

In the library she still couldn't shake off that unseen presence, lurking between the book racks, hiding in the dark projection cubicles. They were working on a new cataloguing system. Besides the monumental paperwork it involved lifting every book, wiping it clean, wheeling it on a trolley to be slotted into its new place. The dust, the smell of glue and printing ink brought back the afternoons in their old house. Gillie would be out with her crowd, and their parents would be in their practice. Their mother and father hardly ever left each other's side; they had studied together, worked in the same GP surgery, and even in death they kept close ranks. Horobin was right, she was angry, her childish belief still intact: had Mummy tried a little harder, she could have stayed with Gillie and Gail a little longer. Rather than deserting them hurrying after Dad.

THIRTEEN

The days had become so gloomy that she had to have the light on all the time. Passing from room to room she would hesitate, in case she glimpsed an unexpected shadow. What if she suddenly spotted an unexpected rip of colour, a black shoe under the wardrobe? *Projective identification*, that's what it was. She thought of phoning someone for company—maybe Annie whom she went to school with. There was also Lyn. But Lyn she hadn't seen for years. Everyone had become used to her being immersed in her studies, they had all stopped counting on her.

For dinner she roasted potatoes, grilled three trout and tracked down a tub of expensive ice cream, in hope that Ben might bring Kiko back with him. She poked at her food in front of the TV. She slept badly, waking every hour, listening for footsteps. Perhaps Ben and Kiko had stayed on somewhere after a party. In the morning she phoned Jimmy Rollo to ask if he happened to know Ben's whereabouts. When Jimmy claimed ignorance she began to panic. What if Ben lay injured in a hospital? Around eleven someone tried to call from a phone booth but failed. Ben had never stayed away this long without telling her, she complained to Eddie on the phone. Only to hear that one day this had to happen. Ben was old enough.

In the afternoon the phone rang and this time it was Ben. Staying for the weekend with Kiko's family, he would be back tomorrow night. And can Gail *please* stop bothering his friends! No one's parents would behave in such an embarrassing way. Later Ben called again: Kiko's dad is taking them to a football match and afterwards cooking a meal for them. Is it all right to stay another night? He'll be back tomorrow after school.

On Monday, after work, Gail waited for him till late. When he finally came, alone for once, he went straight to bed without saying hello.

Back on the couch again. Before lying down Gail scrutinized the cushion for any sign of Volkswagen man's hair, then embarked on her well-rehearsed topic—her fear of something going catastrophically wrong. She expected Horobin to tell her that the disaster she feared had already struck: her parents' death. Then Benny's. They had been through this before. But today Mrs. Horobin came up with a new angle: what Gail feared, she suggested, was the separation from her.

Gail raised herself on her elbow to give Horobin the benefit of her disdain. "Mrs. Horobin, I'm sure there are worse things than separating from your therapist."

It took Horobin some time to react. "This I wouldn't dispute," she finally said. "But I wanted to talk to you about something."

"What?" Gail was still facing her.

Horobin made as if searching for an answer. "What I wanted to say is that your therapy with me might end earlier, Gail."

Gail felt a chilling draught, as if right next to her a freezer's lid had been flung open. Horobin had been disingenuous with her. She lay back and confronted the familiar view: the lamp with its circle of silly tassels and its orange shadow on the liver-red wall, the shelf full of stunted cacti. From behind, she heard Horobin's deep gasps for air, the creaking of the armchair under her weight, sensed her stale warmth. She had to find something to knock on the head this monstrous idea of hers. "But Mrs. Horobin, I still have a year to go in my training."

"I'm perfectly aware, Gail," said her therapist. "Perfectly aware. But the thing is—I might have to retire."

"When?"

"Oh, not for a while yet, at least not for another six months."

This time Gail lifted herself up. "Weren't you suppose to tell me before you took me on? Isn't this unprofessional?"

"I'm sorry, Gail. Awfully sorry. But I hadn't quite anticipated …"

"Are you ill?" Gail asked, though what she wanted to do was to shout, *What about me Mrs. Horobin, haven't you thought of me?*

"We shall have plenty of time to prepare to say goodbye," Horobin said. "But you'll need to look for another therapist. Perhaps with this I can help you."

Gail dropped back. If Horobin ignored her needs she had nothing more to say to her. Shortly before the time was up Horobin said, "It is important, Gail, that we take time to say a proper goodbye. Not to have to cut off like, sadly, you had to with your parents." To let Phyllis Horobin know how unimpressed she was, Gail made a snorting sound. "Or with Ben," added Horobin. *Benny*, Gail corrected her, but only in her head. "Together we'll try … we will try to find a way for you to mourn your loss." Horobin expanded her idea. "To survive it without resentment."

Her loss? The instant the session ended Gail stood up and, staring straight ahead, put one foot in front of the other until she sat in her car, the engine running. Through a blur she watched the plane trees' trunks slip by, their twisted roots lifting the pavement, their grey peeling skin exposing the unsightly lesions underneath. Grey, green—Horobin's colours. She tried to guess the nature of Horobin's illness. Advancing *loss* most probably—she noticed the bitter satisfaction the word *loss* gave her—of the use of her puffed-up legs.

Next time Alena Sokol drove in again by herself. Instead of keeping her coat bundled in her lap she hung it on the back of her chair—signs Gail chose to read as progress. During this session Alena tackled all sorts of topics, except for one: Tata's swimming incident. She mentioned their Prague one-room apartment overlooking an old cemetery. She spoke about Sundays she spent looking at a chair till she believed she herself stood on four legs—Tata's method for teaching her to take photographs was to study something for so long you became the thing itself. Only then was Alena allowed to press the shutter of his East German camera. Tata, on the other hand, snapped thousands of shots of his daughter, which he pasted into large albums. Tzvack tzvack, tzvack, Alena's finger demonstrated: Tata's eyes always on her.

"So how did it feel being observed by your father all the time?"

Familiar silence that usually followed a question.

"Or in fact by anyone else who might be trying to, you know, even these days …" Purposefully, Gail let the sentence trail off.

Alena lowered her gaze, her cheeks full and smooth, the monolithic fringe of her bob shiny as a freshly grilled sausage. Was Alena playing a game with her? They could go on like this forever. Shortly before the end of the session Gail decided to tackle her head on. "By the way, Alena, that day in Butlins you told me about, the day of the Russian invasion when your father went for that swim … What happened then?"

For a moment Alena Sokol just stared at her. Then she turned and yanked her coat from the chair.

"Alena? We still have a few minutes."

82

Alena stuffed her arms through the sleeves. "People here say they're interested. Stay in touch, they say. Drop in … things like this. But they're just being polite."

"Alena, how can you say that? I *am* in touch, I *am* interested!"

Alena glared at her. "Then why," she hissed in a voice thin with rage, "why when I told you Tata was gone, why did you forget?"

Gail shook her head. "I'm sorry, but I wasn't sure what you meant."

"Gone means gone. Means never found."

So she had been right after all; there hadn't been a happy end. Alena Sokol too had been orphaned, the two of them were a fit.

To make lasagne you have to cook four separate things: the pasta, the béchamel sauce, the mince, and the tomato sauce. Then comes the sticky business of heaping the layers on top of each other before shoving the whole lot in the oven. While cooking Gail saw the scene in her head: Alena, alone on the cold wet sand staring at the luminous line the moon has thrown over the black water, tears rolling down her round childlike cheeks and no one to comfort her. Gail laid the table and called Ben.

"Not in the mood for talking, mum." Ben took his plate and installed himself in front of the TV. Happy for his company she sat next to him. Fork to mouth, fork to mouth—Ben shoved the food in at such a breathless tempo, helping it down with loud gulps of Coke, that she worried he might choke. Despite his request he hardly glanced at the screen. Staying at Kiko's was fun, he mumbled, when she enquired. In Kiko's house everyone is easy-going and no one makes a fuss.

"Oh that's nice," she said, suppressing a stab of envy. "So what was that lovely meal Kiko's dad cooked?"

"Nice ... lovely ..." Ben mocked her. "Mum, you're so phoney."

"Sorry," she mumbled. Her face felt hot. Perhaps she had reached the end of her reproductive span. Already? On the screen the newscaster said that Princess Diana was suing the *Daily Mirror* for secretly taking photos of her in the gym. Next, the news from Bosnia: a camera tracked up a dusty village road to where a boy, thirteen at the most, was squatting near some men digging in the ground, handkerchiefs tied over their noses. They had unearthed a small plastic purse. Blue. One man lifted it in the air in a shower of soil. Numbly, the boy gaped at it. But when the man passed the purse to him the boy grabbed it and ran. After a few steps he stopped, bent over, and started to retch. The purse belonged to the boy's fourteen-year-old sister, commented the voice off-camera. Killed by their neighbours.

Not something to watch while having dinner with your son. Your son, only a few years older than that boy. Now that she knew Bosnia had nothing to do with Alena Sokol she was at liberty to switch the channels. But when she glanced back, Ben was asleep on the sofa, clutching the fork. Under the dark brows his long eyelashes still curved as they had when he was little. But for a few teenage spots his skin was glossy. Near his left temple the pale scar from his seaside holiday mishap added to his looks. To Gail, her son seemed astonishingly handsome. Removing the fork from his fingers made her remember how she used to kiss them when they were still cushioned in baby fat. And now those fingers explored another female's flesh. She whispered, "Darling, wake up." He stirred, groaned, but his eyes remained shut. She ran her hand over his soft boyish stubble then slid it behind to rub his back. "Off to the loo and then straight to bed. You can skip brushing your teeth."

"Mum!" Ben scrambled to his feet. "Eat, sleep, shit is all you care about." He staggered to the door. From there he turned, his face suddenly grey. Was this how he will look in twenty years? "You don't really want to know how I feel. Do you?"

She thought of the time when Ben, as an infant, had been sent to Gillian in New Zealand because she, his mother, cracked up. Was she letting him down again? "Oh Ben, darling!" She rushed to him. "Of course I want to know. I want to know everything about you!" She pulled him to her but he wriggled himself free.

"So why don't you ever ask?"

"Because you don't bloody let me!"

He turned away from her but not quick enough: she saw that he was crying. "Kiko dumped me."

Her son had been dumped? How could anyone do this to him? Dumped! The word made her feel second-rate. "But you said how nice it was in Kiko's house. And how her parents ..."

She was met with a look of pity: "I've been staying at Jimmy's mum's. Honestly, I don't know how you can call yourself a therapist."

Twice in the same day she had been accused of failing to notice things. If she couldn't guess her own son's mind, what chance did she have with strangers? But she was training as a therapist, not a clairvoyant.

FOURTEEN

She spotted them on her way from the canteen: two figures at the far end of the corridor, the light flooding in through the glass burning all the details. The woman's face—a blur inside a curtain of straight black hair nearly reaching her elbows, shoulders hunched the way tall women do, wide black trousers draping her limbs. Of the man only his light blue back was partly visible, the rest of him obscured by a column. This was enough to slow Gail down. After a few more steps she decided to make a 360-degree turn. Midway through this unexpectedly demanding manoeuvre something made Eddie glance over his shoulder.

"Oh hello. Let me introduce you. Sophie—Gail." Automatically, Gail stretched out her hand. The hand that met hers felt as if its joints had been loosened.

"Sophie is our new member of staff. She started ... when did you start, Soph?"

Soph. In Gail's throat something instantly mushroomed, making it impossible to swallow.

"Three weeks ago," said Soph, pink splotches seeping up her long neck.

"The two of us have just been comparing notes about the ups and downs of living in more than one place," Eddie explained.

The two of us. Her temples began to throb. It had been several days since she saw Eddie. And now he was standing here with this woman and Gail would have to be blind not to notice how she was looking at him, as if his mere presence was enough to cause a myriad of excitations charging through her lengthy person.

"Sophie's lucky to own a house near Tower Bridge. But she has to sleep on friends' floors while it's being done up." Eddie put Gail in the picture.

"It's my parents' house, they live in South Africa."

"Well, that must be difficult," Gail said, pondering if one of those floors—providing it was a floor only—happened to be in Vauxhall. What now? There was nothing for it but to confront this new situation. "Eddie—it has just occurred to me ..." she said, not having a clue where she was headed but persevering just the same, regardless of the consequences, "what about letting Sophie ... letting her stay in your flat while you're with us over Christmas?"

Eddie stopped fidgeting with his moustache. He looked appalled. Offering his sanctuary to a stranger, has Gail gone mad? She felt shocked by her own recklessness: why make such an absurd offer that she wasn't even in a position to make? But anything seemed preferable to being a passive bystander, a victim to assumptions.

"That's kind of you," said Sophie. "But I'm staying with my aunt over Christmas. My aunt lives near one of the biggest outdoor pools in England, I've already told Eddie."

She thinks the world of him, Gail thought. And she calls him Eddie, which had been only Gail's privilege, everyone else called him Ed. No comfort to her that Sophie's blouse hid a pair of rather meagre breasts and that in her clean scrubbed face her lips were paltry. In fact if anything, Sophie resembled one of those elongated Modigliani women. Was Eddie keen on Modigliani? Gail couldn't recall.

Seven-thirty and she was still in the library. She, the consummate student of emotions, was delaying the moment she would have to face Ben with his fresh sorrow. And Eddie with his new conquest. She entertained herself with a fantasy that she would take a train out of town to somewhere no one knew her, where she would dye her hair, buy a fresh set of clothes, and start a new existence under the name of Eve Cava, a character in a novel she had read as a teenager. Apparently this wouldn't be unusual since, according to the statistics, every year thousands of people did just that—they walked out of their homes never to be seen again.

She got off the bus at her stop. The streets were dimly lit and under her feet the dry leaves made rasping sounds. At the crescent she crossed the road to see her own house. Ben's window was dark but the basement was lit and there was Eddie by the kitchen table, reading. For a moment he looked up and smiled absent-mindedly. The sickle of the moon shone above the rooftops, the holly tree rustled with metallic flapping as white-collared pigeons hung upside down pecking red berries, Christmas decorations made alive. Suddenly the world seemed more welcoming. And then noiselessly, like a long somnambular creature, the Nomads slid into view: the redhead at the helm with her pram, followed by her brood, the father closing the ranks. They passed so near that she could sniff the washing powder on their clothes.

"First time's always hard but he'll survive," was Eddie's response when she told him about the break-up. Apparently Ben had declined dinner and gone straight to his room. She climbed the stairs, stood behind his door then knocked. No answer. She assumed he must be asleep. While she and Eddie ate and even later in bed when Eddie pressed his cold belly to her back, Sophie wasn't mentioned.

She was woken by the phone. "It's Kiko. Sorry for calling so late but I just want you to know that Ben's OK." This girl had a nerve; first she makes her son unhappy and then she calls in the middle of the night. Rather than going back to sleep she went to listen at Ben's door again. Surely Ben wouldn't do "something stupid"? She quietly let herself in. In the pitch dark she stumbled over the things that littered the floor, till her shin banged against the bed. She froze, waiting for Ben to stir. But when the room remained silent she cautiously tapped the bed-cover, gradually working her way up. Then she stopped. Ben wasn't there, that's what Kiko's call was about. She lay down and burrowed her face into the empty mattress.

FIFTEEN

"A suicide?" she repeated after Rudi, with disbelief. "What makes you think Alena's father would take his own life?"

She was squatting in front of the contents of her handbag scattered over the threadbare rug. She had written detailed notes but now she could not find them. Around her, books were precariously piled in dusty towers; every corner grew its own soft ball of flotsam. Plainly, Rudi Chang was too busy with the frailties of the human mind to fit in an occasional housework. "What makes you think Alena's father would commit suicide?"

"Russian invasion was a colossal event, Gail. When such things happen, people break."

"Rudi! He had a daughter to take care of, don't forget." Only someone who had no progeny could think up something so outrageous, so selfish; however much loved, a dog can never substitute for a child, even if you named it after your guru.

"Out of interest, was there an autopsy?"

"The thing is, they never found Alena's father's body."

"Sou-kol's papa never fished from the sea? Ocho! Why didn't you say?"

Today she found her supervisor's comments irritating. The shock she had felt last night on discovering Ben's empty bed was still with her. How do you carry on without knowing your son's exact whereabouts? She had even convinced herself to feel grateful to Kiko for informing her that Ben was safe. She hoped it meant he stayed the night in her house. Or if not in hers, then in Jimmy's.

"And you Gail?" Rudi inspected her with his onyx eyes. "Why you cross?"

She released her jaw. "Cross? Why should I be cross? Look, Alena's father travelled to see her all the way from Prague. He was very possessive, couldn't bear the idea of ever parting from his daughter."

"Uhum ... And then he drowns and poor Sou-kol never buries him. Therefore—never mourns. Burials of tremendous importance, Gail, we know this from catastrophes, from wars."

Watching Rudi scratching his nose with his pen she thought of her parents' grave and that she never went there.

"I'm having better understanding of Sou-kol," Rudi murmured. "She loses both parents but gets a job where things are found."

"Actually," she jumped in, "Alena showed me pictures of some of those things, she photographs them."

This seemed to please Rudi. "She takes photos of lost things? Gail, it is like carving name on a tombstone. But is it allowed? I think Sou-kol feels *ee-noor-mous* guilt."

Gail remembered having a similar thought: that the lurking presence clinging to Alena Sokol's heels was not a physical person, but her guilt.

"We mustn't forget Sou-kol's mother died at her birth," Rudi pursued his thoughts. "Causing your mama's death? Ocho! This hard to live with message! Overwhelming. And afterwards her father dies in the sea ..." Rudi sighed. "You know, Gail, Sou-kol may believe everyone who comes near her dies. That's why her ambivalence about letting you close."

Gail was appalled. "Are you saying that Alena thinks that getting closer to me might cause me to die?"

Rudi's eyebrows shot up. "You must remember, Gail, here we not considering reality. We considering Sou-kol's internal fantasies. People like her sometimes deluded about their special powers." Seeing the incredulity in her face Rudi decided to humour her: "But Sou-kol's husband still alive, isn't he?"

This was absurd. She told Rudi Chang that although her parents were both dead, same as Alena's, it had never occurred to her to think of herself as a guilty culprit.

"Exactly, Gail!" Rudi chuckled. "This the difference between those with ordinary neurosis, like you or me, and those with something more serious."

She was on her way up the stairs when she heard the door: Ben with Kiko in tow, both giggling, poking each other. "Hi," they greeted her, heading straight for Ben's room, the "dumping" all but forgotten.

In her bedroom Eddie was already asleep, a magazine open on his chest. She intertwined herself around him. Then she had a dream: she is in a landscape painted thick with acid greens, toxic yellows, and evil blues. Even while dreaming she knows she abhors those colours. Above a hill a circular object rolls in. Its metal coating makes her shiver. It spins around and aims at her: a cannon. She scurries backwards but the cannon follows her, the muzzle now like a black glistening mouth. Finally it gets closer, so close she can peer inside. Its dark sheen fills her with terror. Then the thing gives a little cough and squeezes out a pink blob. How clever, she thinks, to make the gun endearing. Then it fires. The explosion is like a sunflower shooting into bloom and she expects to be torn apart. Instead, what lands on her left shoulder is hardly heavier than a squirrel.

She woke up drenched and with a distinct sense that the dream with its peculiar aesthetics had arrived to her from some other, alien world.

Today was Alena's penultimate session before the Christmas break and Gail's training has drummed into them that at such times it was paramount to confront the upcoming separation. Separation that was bound to activate feelings of rejection, of sadness and loss.

Far from looking like someone whose mere presence could kill, Alena wore something bland as usual. "Tata comes from Rusovce," she announced as soon as she settled.

"Oh. Is this in Russia?" Here was a surprise.

"No, it's by Dunay. Danube, you call it. When Tata was little his father jumped in Dunay from a bridge."

"His father, your grandfather killed himself?"

But even if Alena's grandfather had committed suicide, it didn't prove Rudi was right. It still didn't mean that Alena's father had wanted to drown himself. Just as it didn't follow that because of Gail's parents' early death she was destined to die young.

"Tata's mother wanted him to be scientist," Alena went on. "For that she named him Nicola." And the connection between being a scientist and being named Nicola? "Tata's mother admired Nicola Tesla." Tesla. Who was Tesla?

Gail's ignorance surprised Alena. Didn't everyone know that Tesla was a famous scientist who worked with electricity? Alena already knew this when she was a child. She knew that Nicola Tesla was from Serbia but ended up in America, where Alena's father was also hoping to go. But there was a war, so instead, Alena's father went to the mountains to fight with the partisans. He was only young but already he spoke Slovak, Czech, Hungarian, and German.

Gail was beginning to have qualms about this new eagerness. Tata Nicola had been dead for years but thinking about him made Alena unusually talkative, recalling all sorts of things: his treasured possession was supposed to be a book of old photographic prints that Alena, as a child, believed to be his family album. The lady in a flowery hat gazing dreamily

93

into the distance, an open letter slipping from her hand, Alena assumed was her grandmother whom she had only met once. The ladies huddled around a small peephole she took for her aunts, though what they saw in there Tata had never said. There was also a wedding picture: the bride in a lacy robe next to the bridegroom in coat-tails, her hand teasing something from his pantaloons, some small object—his handkerchief perhaps. In another photo, the bridegroom hunted for something under his new wife's crinoline.

Erotic Victoriana—they had a similar volume in the college library. But to a child these photos must have been puzzling: a naked couple impersonating a four-legged crab-like creature, a head on each side, biting into its own flesh …? Ladies aiming from under their skirts a playful arc of water into a goblet! Did Alena stumble across these by herself or did her father, in his fervour for early photography, show them to her? How long before Alena deduced that these were not her grandparents, uncles, and aunts?

"So what did you think these people, the people you took to be your family, were up to?"

Alena chewed on her lip. "Tata said it was art."

Tata! Always Tata, as if nothing else mattered in Alena's life, adored even when corrupting Alena. Perhaps Gail's task was to prevent him from colonising their therapy. She glanced at the clock; she still hasn't tackled the Christmas holiday. She did ask Rudi if she could take only a short break but Rudi insisted that a proper break was an opportunity for Alena to start practising mourning. Mourning, that old chestnut!

"Alena, we need to talk about the Christmas break," gently Gail flagged up her topic.

"Talk?" Alena echoed as if this manner of communication still took her by surprise.

"I'm proposing to take two weeks off." In the absence of a reaction Gail handed Alena a piece of paper. "Here's my invoice. And the dates for when we finish and when you come back."

Alena Sokol unfolded the invoice. "So therapy's finished now?" she asked, whether with trepidation or hope Gail couldn't say. She watched Alena's eyeballs move under her eyelids there and back, the fine yellow down on her cheeks shimmer like delicate algae. Still time to call the break off. Therapy happens behind closed doors: Rudi wouldn't have to know. Behind closed doors all sorts of things can go on. Taboo things. Gail has heard stories about therapists having sex with their patients and then having to be struck off by ethics committees. Because in therapy a patient regresses into a childlike state, which puts the therapist in a position of power, like a parent. Sex with your patient was as bad as incest.

"No, we still have one more session—at 6.30 on Tuesday. Please don't forget."

By the door, as Alena passed her without a word, Gail felt a sudden urge to punch her in the back. Or grab her by her shoulders and make her rattle, just to get a reaction. As usual Alena Sokol checked the street: all clear, the white van stood in its place. Her foot already on the doorstep, she suddenly turned and said, "I had a dream last night." In the bright light her cheeks now made Gail think of the surface of a faraway planet. "I ran and there was something after me. A big round thing."

The hour was over and the only thing left to do was to bid her patient goodbye. But Freud had called dreams the royal road to the unconscious and Gail couldn't resist making a step in that direction. At least Thomas wasn't here to witness her misconduct.

"That round thing, what did it remind you of, Alena?"

Alena shrugged. "A gun?"

A gun? Gail tried to hide her disbelief. This was too uncanny to be a fluke. By some baffling, inexplicable means, during last night she and Alena had shared a dream. It was as if Alena had managed to climb inside her head. Or vice versa, both equally disturbing.

SIXTEEN

Over the next few days the leaves lost the last of their sheen. In the window, the bough man became little more than a few emaciated sticks, nothing for the wind to grasp. Since that morning she had first made out his waving arm, she looked for him in the treetops every time she woke up. She got her winter coat from the loft and found a glove in each pocket, like two forgotten friends. The sky continued to be of a solid grey on which no heavenly hand bothered to paint anything. One morning, patches of white covered the garden. Patches of novelty. In an hour they were gone.

On the evening of Alena's last session everyone happened to be in. Through the floorboards Gail could hear Eddie coughing, Ben and Kiko making frequent trips up and down the stairs. She reminded them all again that her patient was due at 6.30 and that it was paramount to keep the house hushed.

At 6.25 she sat in her chair. At 6.45 she was still there, alone. She paced the room, listened to the hiss of the central heating, the tapping of the venetian blind, the crackling of Eddie's newspaper. *People sometimes turn up late, it happens, she should use the time to note down what comes to her mind about Alena; they have been told to do this while waiting for a patient. It may be that the upcoming break is making Alena feel insecure.* Seven o'clock came and went. Outside, silhouettes faded into front doors, late arrivals from work. Probably Alena had got the date wrong. At ten past seven Eddie peeked in. "Still not here?" She waved him away: ten more minutes to go to the end of the session that wasn't taking place. Only when those minutes are over will she mark DNA in her notebook. Did Not Attend. After all the fuss about everyone having to be on their best behaviour she had been made to look a fool. To phone Alena was out of the question: the protocol was, you are not to chase your patient. Now a whole two weeks of holiday would have to pass before she would see Alena again; she should have listened to her instinct, shouldn't have let her go. After losing her mother at the very start, for Alena Sokol any separation had to be traumatic. And what if she never came back?

Just then the phone rang. Gail dashed out and got to it seconds before Eddie. In those few seconds she had decided that after Alena gave her a reason for not turning up, plausible or not, she would offer her an alternative session. And not only that, she would offer to see her throughout the holiday. "It's for me," she mouthed to Eddie. "Alena? Alena, please don't worry that you didn't make it today, it's no problem."

"Can I speak to Eddie please," a female voice said at the other end.

She passed the phone to Eddie. "Hi Soph," he said, leaning into the windowpane as if wanting to vaporise through the glass. The signal couldn't be clearer: he wished to be left alone. She stayed—it was her house after all. Her phone. She sat down and watched his back. And his fine, papery profile. Which of his parents did Eddie look like? His father came from Iceland, his mother was Scottish. Eddie adored his father while his mother he could do without. Sometimes Eddie joked that he instigated his premature birth because he preferred an incubator as his first home. Gail kept straining to hear what was being said but Eddie resorted to questions like "Who?",

"When?", "What?". From the other end she caught a muffled burst of sobs to which Eddie replied: "OK, OK."

"What was all that about?" she asked the moment Eddie hung up.

"Sorry, but it's private." Private? Who would guess who was the therapist around here? Then Eddie changed his mind. "She seems awfully unhappy. She goes for daily swims but at her aunt's it's rather hectic with the dinner parties. It's too much for her."

She forced a laugh. "Poor Soph! Honestly! But why phone you?" When Eddie replied that Sophie had phoned to enquire if she could stay in his Vauxhall flat over Christmas, Gail pulled a face. "But you hardly know her!"

"She is wary of people. I feel sorry for her."

"She doesn't seem wary of you."

"Well, it was your idea after all."

And that was that: Eddie went off to give Sophie the keys to his flat. When he got back Gail was already in bed. They slept as if someone had wedged a slab of ice between them.

In the morning she rang Rudi Chang to ask what to do about Alena Sokol's non-attendance.

"So, Sou-kol didn't come? Write her a letter. Say you regret no coming but looking forward to seeing her after Christmas break."

Ashamed to admit that so far her attempts at extracting Alena's address had resulted in a scribbled phone number, she assured Rudi she would follow his advice.

SEVENTEEN

Colindale was the third stop before the last on the Northern Line. As a librarian she knew about the Newspaper Reading Room though she had never come here before. The sombre structure reminded her of a mausoleum. The security was firm: two forms of identification and an absolute ban on bringing anything inside, except for a piece of paper and a pencil, not even a pen! Her first foray into an unknown territory, the unsafe zone where a psychotherapist turns into a sleuth. She was directed past the cubicles with crouched figures rattling the scanners' wheels. The *Guardian* for the year 1968 came in a small reel of microfilm. She rolled the screen to 21 August, the day of the Russian invasion of Czechoslovakia—news that shocked the world. Slowly, she progressed through the following days: shooting in front of the radio station, several people killed, Dubcek's government kidnapped, flown to Moscow where they were forced to sign a document agreeing with the so-called brotherly help. Then, under the reports from the regions something caught her eye:

DROWNED HOPES. Only hours after the Soviet army occu-
pied their country, the father of a Czech student, one of the
contingent of first time Eastern European recruits working

in Butlins holiday camps, has drowned in a tragic incident in
Bognor Regis.

She rolled on: *Czechoslovak students taken in English homes …*
Unskilled jobs required for Czech students … To raise money for
stranded students Dvorak's Cello concerto in B Minor is being spon-
sored by Czech dissident maestro Rafael Kubelik in the Albert Hall.
About the drowned man there was no further mention.

She went to ask at the desk if Bognor Regis had a local paper.
Of course: the *Bognor Regis Observer*. This time she was given a
box of microfiche. She changed scanners, placed sheets of film
between the glass and pulled them under the lens. And there
it was again:

> *SUNK HOPES: On the same day as Russians invaded Czecho-*
> *slovakia the father of a Czech employee at Butlins Holiday*
> *Camp in Bognor Regis has drowned when taking a swim*
> *in the sea. His daughter, one of 80 Czechs and Slovaks who*
> *obtained visas to work in Butlins this year, was too distressed*
> *to comment, though her fiancé said they will not return to their*
> *country till her father is found. Billy Butlin offered the grief-*
> *stricken employee personal condolences and one week's stay free*
> *of charge.*

A fiancé? In a group photo of identical overcoats, she recognised the young Alena: long dark hair, no fringe to speak of.
The bearded youth next to her she made out as Thomas. When
did these two manage to get engaged? And why didn't Alena
mention that Thomas had also worked in Butlins?

Searching out details about your patient, she knew she was
breaking the rules. Yet here she was, secreted away in a dark
cubicle, rushing magnified print under her eyes, not minding
the ventilation blowing in icy air. She stayed till they closed,
then, shivering, emerged into the evening drizzle. The smell of

food from a Turkish café across the road reminded her she had not eaten all day.

It was warm inside. She ordered something small and was asked to pay in advance. Within minutes a selection of trays appeared in front of her, far more than she could consume.

"No problem," the owner joked. "What you don't eat I give you next time."

She wasn't likely to be back, she said.

"Then fortunately it won't rain again." When she looked at him puzzled, the man repeated: "Then unfortunately I won't see you again." With Alena Sokol it was similar: you hear one thing, then there is something else.

She marvelled about why Alena had kept quiet about Thomas. Did Alena's father know about him? Was Thomas the reason he had travelled to England? Has something happened between them, an argument? Perhaps more.

Customers trickled in, picked up their takeaways and left. On hearing a familiar voice order a diet Coke, properly chilled, Gail looked up: a flick of blonde hair above an upturned collar: Karla Urbanova. What a mad, mad coincidence that they should bump into each other, here of all places.

Gail? Karla had already spotted her. Karla! What you doing here? Karla pointed outside: I do surveys for Chris's law firm of what was in the papers on such and such a date. And you? Research for my library.

The next thing she knew she was sitting in Karla's BMW heading for Archway where Karla was to drop her off to catch the Tube. In her black leather gloves with cut-off fingers Karla handled the wheel with brisk nonchalance. "Your Czech woman, has she started speaking?" Not waiting for an answer Karla went on about her own patients, two women, both chatty. One was coming to Karla because her boyfriend left her for a man. The other had many medical problems, such as strong perspiration. "Please!" Karla smiled and in exasperation momentarily let go off the steering wheel. "In this business everyone's so damn self-centred, including us. I tell you, those ethnically cleansed Yugoslavs, now they have something to perspire about."

Chatty patients with simple, clear-cut symptoms—some people were lucky. Gail felt dizzy and wished she was back home. Yet when Karla invited her to her home she instantly accepted. To spend time in the company of someone from Alena Sokol's country, she wasn't to let such an opportunity pass.

A lift took them to the top floor of a modern block. Behind the front door, pairs of shoes were lined up under spotlights like flowers in a patch. The hall opened into a wide space: a few choice pieces of furniture, rugs on pine floorboards, one wall made entirely out of glass. Beyond, a terrace with a view of the London night sky.

"Should I take my shoes off?" Gail asked.

"If you want." Karla passed her oriental-looking leather slippers decorated with silk knots. Her own heels she kept on. Perched at each end of an L-shaped sofa, sipping strange-tasting liquor from angular glasses that Karla pointed out were an original Czech cubist design, they looked as if they were posing for a stylish magazine. At least Karla did, with her impressive bone structure, her strong teeth, and athletic legs, her ponytail pulled high. Gail felt she urgently needed to lose a few pounds and have her roots done.

"When does Chris get home?" she enquired, just to say something. It did cross her mind that Karla might see her with the same critical eye she herself had reserved for Alena. How would Alena Sokol feel amid all this elegance? Except for some hard-to-specify bluntness, these two didn't seem to have much in common.

"Chris? Not till late. They keep them busy at the firm."

Gail had already used the bathroom and noticed that no male toiletries were in view. Perhaps Karla and Chris had a similar arrangement as she and Eddie, with Chris having his own place.

"It's not that I don't like the theory." Karla returned to their car conversation. "The theory is great. But it's not proper science, is it? It's more like something you make up as you go. How about you? Do you know how to put it all into practice?"

Here was Gail's chance to bring Alena Sokol in again. "Me? Well, I've only just started. My patient told me she came here in 1968. I don't think she's ever gone back."

"Well, if you went back they wouldn't let you out again. Not till after the Velvet Revolution, and that's only five years ago."

"So how did you come to England?"

"Got married."

"To Chris?"

"No, to someone else."

A somewhat abrupt response but it allowed Gail to return to Alena. "When the invasion happened my patient was already here in England. Her father came to see her. But he drowned in the sea."

Karla made a shocked face. "He drowned! And she?"

"She waited for him to be found. But he never was." Gail thought of telling Karla about Thomas and how he unexpectedly popped up in that photo, but then she changed her mind. "I don't think Alena was completely alone, there were other Czechs around. They organised a concert of Czech music to raise money for those stranded in England. A cello concerto in the Albert Hall."

Karla thought for a moment. "Probably Dvorak. Not that many Czech geniuses, but Dvorak's one of them. And Janacek of course." She got up to inspect the CD rack. "We've got lots of Dvorak. Here—Dvorak's Cello Concerto in B Minor. Would you like to hear it?"

B Minor. It sounded like the one they had mentioned in the *Guardian*. Before Gail had a chance to say anything, Karla slotted the CD in, slipped out of her heels, and folded her black-stockinged legs. After the opening, sombre and slow, the violins started their pursuit. Then the other instruments announced a theme. The violins picked it up and in no time the melody swelled up into something grand. Hoping not to look too serious Gail shut her eyes. She would have preferred to watch the city lights but did not dare to turn away from Karla. She even swayed a little, wondering if Alena Sokol was familiar with this music. Not very likely Alena visited the Albert Hall while she waited for her father to turn up. When Gail opened her eyes again Karla's place was empty, only the shoes had stayed. Now the violins became more intimate, sounding like they were demanding something, a pressing question. Through their tremulous pleading Gail tried to discern Karla's movements around the flat. When Karla returned she wordlessly offered Gail a bowl of almonds. Gail put a few in her mouth but, afraid of making crunching sounds, only sucked on them. Now the clarinets, or maybe they were oboes, chatted to each other and then, unexpectedly, a cello took over. It turned into a wounded human voice, it sang and ached. Gail caught Karla's gaze yet her expression didn't give anything away. "Shall I stop it now or would you like to hear some more?" Karla asked after the cello solo was over.

Gail said it was beautiful but she'd have to be heading back. While she put her shoes on Karla lifted the CD out of the deck. "Here, have it." Gail wasn't sure whether to take it but Karla said not to worry, they had two: one by Casals and this one by Rostropovich.

"But what about Chris? He might want to have them both."

Karla examined her face. "She. Chris is a she, and she won't miss it."

Chris. Christine? Gail blushed, blurting out she didn't know. No matter, Karla said, she didn't advertise it. Though this was

104

the main reason why she had left. To be a lesbian back home? No thanks, people there were backward, unbelievably so.

Gail listened to the CD while she cooked. And also later with her eyes shut. The high tones cut straight into her, especially the flutes; they had the power to draw something immense: a sky, two tiny figures on a beach—Alena and her father. Or were they three? Was Thomas there watching Tata struggle in that heavy swell? The cello's startling insistence, was it more like a lover's plea or a father's complaint? Or a lament of guilt? She waited for when the cello began to weep, leaden with sorrow, then stopped the music and picked up the phone. After one ring only there was a voice:

"Thomas Smutny." Too late to hang up now.

"This is Gail May. Can I please speak to Alena?"

"Miss May, the therapist?"

How many Miss Mays could Thomas possibly know? "Is Alena there please?"

Alena was with Danusha, Thomas said. Danusha hasn't been well. Was it something urgent?

No, she said. But since she hadn't seen Alena last week she wanted to make sure Alena knew when they were starting after the break. None of Thomas's business, of course, when Alena was booked to see her, but it was too late to stop now. And who was Danusha?

"Apologies for the missed session but we had to bring Danusha from the home and Alenka had to take time off work. Danusha is staying with us over Christmas." Thomas paused. "Alenka told you about our daughter?"

"Of course," she said, in a matter-of-fact voice. "I hope she'll get better soon."

"By the way, you charging for missed sessions?"

Sounding priggish even to herself she said she could only discuss this with Alena.

105

So Alena Sokol had a daughter: for this nothing had prepared Gail. While Alena rumbled on and on about Tata Nicola, not a word about her child, not a squeak. A daughter who had to live in a home and for whose wheelchair, most probably, their Ford had had to be adapted.

EIGHTEEN

M ore unprecedented developments concerning Eddie's apartment: a tap needed tightening, one of the kitchen cupboards wouldn't close, and a bird opened its bowels on the windowpane, each emergency requiring Eddie's personal assistance. Every time Eddie returned from his mission he looked more tense. One evening when he came back later than usual she confronted him: "What're you doing, spending all this time with Sophie?"

"What am I doing? You invite her to stay in my flat and now you're asking me?"

"Yes! Why can't Sophie deal with any of this herself?"

"She needs her energy for her swims." Was Eddie serious? When she glared at him, he cradled his head and she noticed, for the first time, a patch of skin showing through his fair hair. "She lives out of boxes and there isn't a scrap of food in the fridge. Seems I have a bloody nutter on my hands."

She bent over and kissed that ash-pink place where newborns still have a bone to grow. Whenever she saw Eddie in front of the flickering screen, the computer humming its inhalations, its coolings, Gail imagined this to be the nearest he got to replicating his incubator life. She had an image of him when finally brought home with nothing but a blanket to protect him from the rawness of the air and the human clamour; he must have received a brutal jolt. An awakening that would mark him for life; on her course they have devoted hours to child development. It seemed that the attraction of the pale, loose-limbed Sophie was that she carried a similar air of hurt.

After a conciliatory entanglement on the sofa, then through semi-clad retreat to the bedroom, they hatched a brand new plan: after Sophie left Eddie would put his flat on the market and move in with Gail. On a permanent basis. This unprecedented, for Eddie an almost kamikaze-like act, was based on a revolutionary concept: they would build a studio for him in Gail's back garden, one of those wood-panel-and-glass structures you can erect in days.

To Mrs. Horobin Gail chose not to mention Sophie; only that Eddie was moving in with her. Horobin's interpretation—that because of the upcoming Christmas break Gail was trying to replace her with Eddie—Gail shrugged off. Despite having been told how necessary it was to fully experience the pain in these partings, she refused to suffer any.

Today, the girl who had been doing Gail's hair wore on her head red velvet antlers. So close to Christmas Gail was lucky to get a slot with her. They agreed on a shorter cut and some highlights to make a change.

"Doing anything special for Christmas?" the girl quizzed her, throwing a towel over Gail's shoulders, securing it with a sharp clip under her throat. Just the usual, Gail replied. "Special wishes for presents?" The girl energetically stirred the noxious-looking purple paste. Not really. And you? "New tattoo. I already have four but once you start you can't stop, can you?"

Gail closed her eyes and let herself be handled by the girl's competent hands. She liked this girl who did everything 150 per cent. Her thoughts went to Alena and her daughter. Why had Alena kept her secret? What was wrong with her that she couldn't live at home? When she looked up again her hair was lighter than usual, almost honey blonde. And she had a fringe.

Twenty minutes later she stood under a chain of winking lights, pressing Rudi Chang's bell. There was the usual scuffle before the door opened.

"Gail?" Rudi gaped at her.

She shook her new bob. "Who else are you expecting for supervision? A ghost?"

But she couldn't shake off a feeling that in a matter of an hour she had made a home in someone else's skin. The other matter was that not to get entangled in what she knew from Alena Sokol, and through her own findings, she had to perform for Rudi Chang something of a tightrope act. Not that she had little to report: on the contrary. Yet her main scoop, the existence of Danusha, she had to keep to herself. That she had heard about this from Thomas rather than from Alena, Rudi could judge as unethical: a breach of confidentiality he may feel obliged to pass to her teachers. Thomas's presence in Butlins she also had to keep quiet, for fear of exposing yet another instance of subterfuge.

"I can now put you more in the picture about Alena's father," she offered.

Rudi reached for his notepad.

"As a teenager, during the war Alena's father joined the partisans." Rudi nodded, looking impressed. "And afterwards, when Alena's mother died, he had to take care of Alena all by himself, washing, cooking, all that—he and Alena lived alone. But of course now and then he brought a woman in. Alena didn't know why."

"Jealousy painful emotion, Gail," Rudi interjected, hunting around his desk for a pen. Some news!

"Sometimes Alena would find something. Like a slip."

"A slip?"

"A bit of underwear. Or a perfume. Once she found a hair so long that she thought it was a wire."

Rudi crinkled his forehead. "For someone not speaking, these surprising details, Gail."

"Well, she speaks now. She told me she was puzzled about what went on between her father and these women. But most of the time they didn't come back."

"Unfortunately for Sou-kol! Her murderous wishes coming true."

She gawped at him. "Alena's murderous wishes?"

"Just think, Gail, the omnipotent fantasy of killing her rival, her mama, coming true again and again."

She felt nauseous. Karla was right: there was something warped in this way of thinking. Everything in her baulked; Alena was just a regular person, not some theoretical construct. If she couldn't admit to Rudi Chang how close she felt to Alena, Alena who had carried in her belly a daughter just as she had carried Ben, what was the point of being here? She might just as well find something for Rudi Chang to prattle on by himself.

"You know, Rudi," she said à propos of nothing, "I've been listening lately to Dvorak."

Rudi Chang bit the bait instantly. "Antonin Dvorak? Ocho! Sou-kol listens to him?"

Not that Gail knew. But it occurred to her, she told Rudi, she might find in Dvorak's music the sounds of Alena Sokol's mother tongue.

"Sou-kol's mother tongue?" Rudi smiled. "Gail, you trying too hard. But it's true, when Dvorak lived in America, he missed his country, like all immigrants. You familiar with his opera *Rusalka*? The beautiful water spirit who falls in love with a prince but homesick for her lake?" Blinking his sharp eyelids Rudi broke into a nasal chant: "Moon moon on the deep deep sky, this world you wander by ..."

As if in response to Rudi's mournful lament a noise emanated from inside the house and before Gail could make out what it was the door flew open and Gustav hurled himself on his master. He mopped his face with his tongue before turning his attention to Gail—the only possible culprit of his master's distress. Two black powerful paws crashed on her, a pair of eyes bulged above the sharp fangs and she was hit by Gustav's gamy breath.

While Rudi Chang manoeuvred his dog out of the room she tried to calm herself. On Rudi's return she interrupted his apologies to announce that Alena Sokol had a daughter who couldn't live at home and was possibly in a wheelchair and that Gail had learned this through a telephone conversation with Alena's husband. So culpable did Rudi feel for Gustav's misconduct that not only did he not criticise Gail, but rather than concentrating on Alena's *narcissistic wound* due to her bearing a less than perfect child, he conveyed nothing but human sympathy for her.

And her new hairstyle? Dancing a little jiggle around her Kiko deemed it *fringy*. Ben offered her a gel to make the ends spikier and Eddie nuzzled her neck, now exposed under her short-ened hairline. He reported that as soon as Christmas was over Sophie had agreed to vacate the flat. In the meantime Eddie brought over his desktop computer, his anglepoise lamp, and the pneumatic swivel chair. A few days later, one night when they made love, she felt inside her as if something had slotted gently into place. And Eddie, as if to verify it, reached for her foot and squeezed it.

NINETEEN

Despite the break, on Tuesdays and Fridays she looked out for the white van. On Christmas shopping trips she would glimpse a blonde fringe in the shop window and her heart would leap before she recognised herself. While searching for CDs for Ben she looked up *Rusalka* although buying it would be a step too far; she never went to the opera and even on TV rarely managed to follow one till the end. In any case, Alena Sokol had never mentioned Dvorak or *Rusalka*. But then she had never mentioned she had a daughter. Besides buying for Gillie and her husband Frank in New Zealand to whom she sent a yearly parcel, and Ben and Eddie for whom she got the regular things, she bought a hat for Kiko in Gap. She had stopped herself short of getting a present for Kiko's sister Afua whom she had never met, but instead got one for Mrs. Horobin—a magnifying reading lens with a light. She felt she had riches to give; the time for her period came and there was no trace of blood.

At Sainsbury's she picked a turkey big enough to feed at least ten. Eddie viewed Christmas solely as a source of kitsch so it had been left to her to provide merrymaking and togetherness. She asked if Ben wanted to invite Kiko for Christmas dinner. To her surprise Ben agreed, providing they started early so that he and Kiko could then advance to Kiko's house where they ate their dinner late. So now they were four. At some point there was a possibility that Gillie and Frank might come over from Auckland. Gail started to look forward but then Frank hurt his back and they cancelled their trip. Her friend Annie, who with her daughter had had dinners with them in the past, rang to say that this year they were flying to Thailand. Now that Gail and Eddie had made concrete plans about their future together she offered to invite Sophie. But when Eddie said no, Gail didn't insist. Next day, on hearing that Sophie had declined her aunt's invitation, she renewed hers. And via Eddie, received a tentative yes. Now they were provisionally five.

The streets around them had emptied. Even the Nomads came by only once, lugging a plastic shopping bag each, even the kiddies, their dad—the black king closing the ranks, a tree slung over his shoulder—like in a procession of magi. She thought of Alena dressing the Christmas tree, her daughter whizzing around in her wheelchair, making a nuisance of herself. Another two weeks before she would see Alena Sokol again. Before she would put to the test her hypothesis: *Whoever you think is after you, Alena, may not be a real person*, she will say. *We could think of it as your guilt, your old guilt for your mother's dying on you—her baby. And for your father's drowning. None of it is your fault, Alena, just a reminder of your childhood trauma.* Hopefully, once this became embedded in Alena's consciousness she would give up her irrational fear of being followed. Not at once of course, that would be pure fantasy, but gradually, by small advancements, she would free herself from her paranoia.

On Christmas Eve, on a sudden impulse she phoned Karla Urbanova. Skipping the niceties she went straight to the point. "Just wondered if by any chance you and Chris are free tomorrow."

"You're inviting us for Christmas dinner?" Karla checked.

"Yes. Please come and help us to eat our turkey."

Though Karla sounded touched, it turned out Czechs celebrated their Christmas on the same eve Brits besieged the pubs. On that eve Czechs ate carp they bought alive from wooden barrels, potato salad made with real home-made mayonnaise, and a choice of home-baked cookies flavoured with genuine vanilla pods. Then they lit real candles on a real tree and unwrapped their presents. Later still, if there happened to be a church, preferably baroque, they pulled on their warm boots and waded through the snow to sing carols at midnight mass, the air fuzzy with frankincense. In short, Karla and Chris were about to sit down to their festive fish right now. And tomorrow morning they were off to Marrakesh.

One telephone conversation and such wealth of detail. Instantly she saw the scene: Alena laying the table with starched linen and Bohemian crystal, fussing around her daughter, picking the fish bones for her (how old was Danusha?), the whole house infused with hot wax and vanilla.

Christmas Day. The turkey was resting, the roast potatoes glistened in their skins, the sprouts were crunchy, and the carrots sweated in their glaze. The presents had been unwrapped and approved. This year Eddie had taken charge of the tree, rejecting their old decorations in favour of a snake of blue lights and nothing else. Kiko used the occasion to show off her lovely shoulders in an elastic tube top. Ben marked it by wearing his sweatshirt inside out.

Gail surveyed their little gang, each of them here because of her, one way or another. You start as one and then, through your own flesh, you make your pack. This pack of hers, who knows, it might soon expand further, however improbable that seemed. Even the anticipation of Sophie, due any minute after her swim, added to her bliss.

The phone rang while Eddie was carving the turkey. "If it's Kiko's mum," Ben called, "just say we'll be there in two hours."

The arrogance of youth! As if the world had nothing to care about but their arrangements. As if, for instance, this couldn't be Alena Sokol calling to apologise for her recent absence and to wish Gail happy Christmas.

The woman at the other end sounded troubled. "Hello, I'm sorry I'm late but can you please get Eddie?"

As usual, to hear Sophie addressing Eddie this way grated on her. "I'm afraid he's busy right now. Can I help?"

"I just came back from the pool and found a moth in the shower. Not the small one. The nightmoth."

A nightmoth? This grown-up woman was calling to complain about a moth. "We're waiting for you, Sophie, everything is ready. I'm sure by the time you get back it'll be gone."

"But I must shower," the voice insisted.

Gail took the phone to Eddie in the kitchen and while he went on sotto voce she transferred the food onto serving plates. From what she had overheard, despite showering already at the swimming pool it was imperative that Sophie showered again, if only the moth didn't prevent her. Eddie offered Sophie an alternative: she calls a cab, comes over, and showers in their bathroom. "It's OK with you, isn't it?" he checked with Gail.

They decided to start. To make inroads into the bird she carved for everyone a double portion. As Kiko and Ben looked on Ben pointed to the chair waiting for Sophie. "Did you know that in Eastern Europe they keep an empty plate on the table at Christmas on purpose? They told us at school."

Though Kiko claimed this to be a Polish habit, Gail instantly had an image of Alena keeping an empty plate for Tata, year after year, Christmas after Christmas. When the phone rang for the second time Kiko whispered, "If it's Ben's stepdad's friend again, it's so rude. You should never ask her back." *Stepdad*, something Eddie had never aspired to.

"Can I speak to Mr. Edward Berg?" Gail heard a male voice. An official-sounding voice phoning on Christmas Day.

"Who am I speaking to please?"

"St. Thomas's Hospital, A & E. We have a young lady here going by the name of Miss Sophie Peinke. Mr. Berg, he's her next of kin?"

Everyone is gone; the partly exposed turkey carcass looks as if a scavenger has abandoned it in the middle of a feed; the residue of the pudding like something that had dropped out of its gut. After Eddie hurried off, Ben and Kiko also bade Gail a hasty goodbye. They couldn't wait to get to Kiko's house, couldn't wait to tell them the story. *Retelling*, Gail comforted herself, is the best way for those kids to deal with their shock. The shock of hearing that on her way to their Christmas dinner Ben's mum's partner's friend had emptied half a bottle of pills into her mouth in the back of a taxi.

TWENTY

The idea was to spend a weekend in a nice B & B by the sea, just the two of them. Gail even bought a new nightie, silk with lace. And, by pure chance, Bognor Regis was just a stone's throw away. She didn't mention to Eddie what had happened there, that would have revealed too much. Only that her Czech patient worked there in Butlins in the year the Russians had invaded Czechoslovakia. Surely there was nothing wrong in Eddie knowing where her patient came from. That's funny, Eddie said—he had a friend who at that time fell for a Czech girl; Eddie still remembered her name—Mila. He had a vivid memory listening with his friend and Mila to her country's leader sobbing on air with shame. Something Eddie would never forget. Gail felt pleased that Eddie had had a connection with Alena Sokol's homeland long before the two of them had met. Only now in the car, there were not two but three. Could Sophie come?, Eddie had asked at the last minute. Getting out of London after her suicide attempt would do her good. What suicide attempt?, Gail wanted to protest. If you're serious about killing yourself you choose somewhere more private than a London cab.

In her washed-out jean jacket barely reaching her waist, her hair tucked inside a ridiculous fake fur collar that constricted the movement of her head, Sophie looked like a child who had grown too fast. She folded herself in the back seat and kept up an under-the-breath commentary on the passing landscape, her life's ennui miraculously forgotten. Eddie, usually allergic to this sort of a chat, rewarded her with supportive glances. He had told Gail that in the hospital where they pumped Sophie's stomach, they recommended that she should find a psychotherapist. Thankfully, this was none of Gail's business.

To locate Butlins was not a problem: an assembly of low-rise buildings, of bits of fairgrounds and oversized Disney plaster figurines at the east end of the town's sprawl. They parked in a car park just as a toy train trundled in and dumped its clientele of elderly folks. The faithful campers to whom a quarter of a century earlier Alena Sokol had served their Horlicks? Behind the steel fence some noisy youngsters, hair wet from a swimming pool, were squeezing beer cans, steam rising from their naked arms. *The English are a tough breed*, Alena must have thought.

"We're not going in there, are we?" Sophie sounded apprehensive.

"Look, Sophie is tired, we're all hungry, let's go to the beach and have our picnic," Eddie said. When Gail suggested that he and Sophie went ahead first, they both appeared relieved.

The security guard, a lad too young to have been around the night Alena Sokol smuggled in Tata, demanded to see Gail's wristband, a proof that she had bought a day pass. If not, there was the office at the other side. Through the fence Gail glimpsed an arcade with gambling machines and further on of chalets with outside metal stairs, like army barracks. From one of these Alena Sokol and Tata had emerged on the morning their country had been overrun by Warsaw Pact tanks. That same day, Alena climbed back up one of these dismal staircases alone. What else did Gail need to see?

She found them sheltering at the back of boulders overgrown with seaweed: two pale foreheads, two longish faces, both with eyes shut. The hazy sun cast everything in sharp focus, every pebble, every kink in their delicate skin. Years ago another couple had come here: Alena Sokol and her father. Or perhaps they were also a trio, together with bearded Thomas whose presence Alena had kept to herself. Or not a trio—a triangle. The same as now, Gail being the odd one out. To lift one of those heavy stones and smash it on one of those pale foreheads, Sophie's to start with, then Eddie's … With thoughts like these, was she fit to be a therapist?

Gail laid down a tea towel and put on it her spread—stuffed devilled eggs, a bowl of potato salad made with commercial mayonnaise, but still. She distributed plastic cutlery and paper plates. Being on the beach brought new thoughts. What if something different than what Alena had claimed had taken place here all those years back? In the moment of national tragedy Tata demands that Alena breaks with her "fiancé" and returns home with him. An altercation ensues; maybe more: a violent scuffle between the older and the younger man. And then …? Then the guilt stalking Alena might not be purely metaphorical.

She and Eddie ate while Sophie, who contributed a tin of sardines, merely lapped the oil from it as if she were a thirsty dog. It left a greasy trickle on her chin for which Eddie handed her his handkerchief. Then he took out his sketchpad.

The sky remained icy clean, the boulders, as still as a herd of sleeping buffaloes, kept the wind away. Ahead of them, by the glimmering sea's edge some people darted around laughing. One of them took his clothes off and ran into the water, to the cheer of his friends.

"Gosh that guy's brave. It must be freezing," Eddie said.

"If you swim every day you get used to the cold," Sophie replied.

"Yes, but that's not the same as swimming in a pool."

"If it's not heated it's just the same."

"Really?" Gail said. "Could *you* swim in the sea now?"

Sophie smiled. "I don't see why not."

"Well, we wish you wouldn't, don't we?" Eddie sent Gail a look. But she chose not to notice.

"The thing is ..." Sophie now dragged her words, "I don't have a swimsuit."

Eddie rolled his eyes with relief and went back to his drawing. In the distance the figure strolled out from the water as if it were a summer's day. The wind carried to them his friends' applause.

"Actually I have it." Sophie produced a one-piece costume from her bag. "After my swim this morning I forgot to take it out."

Eddie shot another pleading glance to Gail. "Sophie, I don't think this is a good idea, we're not in Johannesburg."

Dangling the costume Sophie marched forward, her sharp buttocks catching the fabric, her black trousers flapping in the wind, like funeral flags, Gail thought. There was nothing to do but to follow her to where the pebbles turned into fine sand. Here, Sophie took off her shoes and socks, her chalk-white feet creating miniscule landslides. While undressing she gazed ahead, as if hypnotised by the foamy expanse in front of her. Every item of clothing she took off she meticulously folded. "Please Sophie, please, this is silly," Eddie repeated into her back. Unsure of her role Gail silently followed the procedure. Was she becoming an accomplice in Sophie's folly simply by standing there, saying nothing? "Silly and dangerous," Eddie kept on with his refrain. Yet Sophie was doing this exclusively for him, Gail could tell. This ghostly girl with her long medusa hair sent out to him her invisible tendrils.

When Sophie got to her panties, not out of modesty but as a protest Eddie strode angrily away, followed by a flock of hysterically weeping seagulls. Oblivious to his departure Sophie took off her bra and knickers. Her stomach was hollow; her thighs no fatter than her arms. Only the other day Gail had

120

seen in a newspaper similar figures in a camp somewhere in Bosnia.

But this was something else, the signs were all there. Anorexics, self-harmers, creatures so weak that anyone who strays into their orbit they suck in. Gail had read innumerable papers on the subject and now she felt the dread of what she was about to witness. All she had to do was say, *It's not worth it, he isn't even looking.* She could help Sophie pull her clothes back on. She could even say, have him if you want, after all people give much more to save strangers. But studying the ins and outs of the human soul didn't guarantee you became an altogether better person. Gail watched Sophie balancing on one foot, then on the other, struggling to get into her damp swimsuit, her skin gritty with goose pimples, her nipples like two rubber plugs. She watched Sophie wading into the icy water, wavering, her back stiffening against the onslaught. If something awful were to happen Gail too would have to live with the guilt, like Alena Sokol. Yet she watched Sophie letting herself sink into the yellow froth, her long hair spreading in a dark slick.

They drove back to London in silence. Wrapped in Eddie's jacket Sophie shivered all the way. More worryingly, her teeth kept on chattering and her lips remained blanched. And yet— they were carting back a living, breathing person, whereas Alena Sokol had left Bognor Regis empty-handed. They passed by Gail's house first so that Eddie could drop her off. As he lifted the rest of the picnic out of the boot their eyes met. "You've changed," he said.

"Have I?" She wanted to ask him what he meant. Not her hair, she knew that, and her period was only a week late, too early to show anything. So she only said, "Well, maybe it's you who has changed."

The look Eddie returned her was of someone pleading for help. "I won't be long," he whispered, his mouth touching her cheek. "I'll just drive Sophie back to the flat."

Gail kissed him back. Under his moustache his lips tasted of salt.

The moment she got into bed she fell asleep as if thrown into a bottomless pit. Around midnight she heard movement on the stairs—Ben and Kiko back early, considering it was Saturday night. But before she had time to start wondering about Eddie she was out again, dreaming that from between her legs her hand was scooping out a mushy substance reeking of peaches. When Gail woke up next it was as if that boulder she had imagined smashing on Sophie's and Eddie's heads had landed on her chest. Eddie wasn't back.

In the morning, when he phoned he sounded cautious. "I'm needed here I'm afraid. Sophie's running a high fever."

"Is she now?"

"Please don't make it more difficult. She is all alone."

Already she had done some crying and now she was angry. She should have made her demands on Eddie earlier, years earlier. But then she had assumed Eddie was incapable of going out of his way for anyone. Now he was proving her wrong. Now that it was too late and that the weak were the ultimate victors. The weak? Since when had she begun counting herself among the strong? Gail put the phone down and he didn't call back.

TWENTY-ONE

Christmas was over and still the shops stayed closed for days and the streets remained empty; even the Nomads must have retreated into hibernation. Bare and thorny, nature seemed at its ugliest. Every day on waking she had to wrestle herself back into life. When her period came she sobbed for a whole afternoon. Just as well there was no one around to pretend to.

"You all right, mum?" Ben asked when she bumped into them in the kitchen one night.

"Yes," she said. "Have I changed?"

"Sure," Ben said, delving in the fridge. He passed Kiko a pot of hummus. "You're less uptight, now that Ed's not around."

"More cool," Kiko agreed. "More independent."

"Cool's the word," Ben said, granting her shoulder a friendly slap.

So much for those who were supposed to know you best.

Alena Sokol's session was four days away. Gail decided that now was the time to phone her to confirm their next appointment; she saw no harm in that. But it was Thomas again who answered the phone. "Nice of you to call. How was your Christmas?"

How odd to hear Thomas's voice, now that she had speculated about his role in Alena's father's demise. Calmly, she asked to speak to Alena.

"Yes, of course, but there's something I need to talk to you about. It's rather ... how should I put it? Tricky."

"I'm sorry but I can only speak to Alena," she insisted.

"Hope you don't think me rude, but since it's you who called you've no choice but speak to whoever picks up."

This time she wasn't going to be drawn in. "If I can't speak to Alena perhaps would you'd be kind enough to—"

"What I want to tell you, if you'd let me ... well, assuming that my wife hasn't mentioned it herself ..."

She wished she hadn't made that call. She shouldn't have. What if Thomas was to confide in her something she shouldn't know? How far was her confidentiality supposed to stretch? Since that day in Bognor Regis she had embellished the scene: three figures on the beach yelling, fighting with each other ... The actual words she doesn't catch and anyway they are in another language. The two men stagger into the splattering tide while the woman frantically scuttles to and fro, overseen by a flock of noisy seagulls. What follows then—the struggle, the muffled cries—she leaves discreetly off-screen.

"By the way, we have to cancel the next appointment," Thomas said. "Possibly also the following two or three. As we're cancelling well ahead I hope you won't charge us."

An instant relief was followed by an instant sense of doom: after Alena's missed session before Christmas, she would now miss a further four. Or perhaps even more. In despair Gail leant against the windowpane, much like Eddie did when he had listened to Sophie on the phone.

"What I was about to tell you, though I don't like saying this because it makes my wife sound mad ..." Thomas's voice bore into her like a poisonous insect. Was he testing her if she would cut the conversation short? On the roofs opposite the chimneystacks held their red accusatory fingers to the sky. You have listened to him far too long, they said. Thomas lowered his voice. "I suppose Alenka didn't tell you, did she, that she actually believes her father is alive."

"But wasn't she there when he drowned?" The words tumbled out of her.

"Yes. But he's never been found, has he?"

She must regain her boundaries, her neutrality. "I'm sorry but I have to end this conversation right now. As I've told you, I can only speak to your wife, so if she isn't there—"

Thomas's voice now quivered with barely suppressed rage. "Excuse me, but what are you? A robot? I've just told you something extremely serious and all you're interested in is—is my wife in or out? By the way, I suppose you're not aware that the word robot—"

Time to stop, to keep to her professional framework, her code of ethics. Would Miranda Green continue lending her ear to this? Would Phyllis? Once more she reiterated that she was not at liberty to discuss her patient with anyone, not even her husband. And if Alena wasn't able to speak to her could Thomas kindly let her have their address so that she can write to her directly?

"You don't give a damn about my wife's state of mind. Her mental health, do you …?" He relished her stunned silence.

She could do nothing but wait. Every passing day chipped at her hope of Alena Sokol ever returning to her. About the likelihood of Eddie coming back she purposefully kept her mind blank. Her dictionary told her *denial* is a defence mechanism by which *a painful experience is repudiated* or *a part of oneself is cancelled out*. Anything wrong with using a bit of each till you get back on your feet? She moved through the house, touched bits of furniture as if seeing them for the first time, or just sat in her room. She inspected her face in the mirror, checking it was still there. She ruminated about Alena's supposed belief that Tata was alive. Why on earth would she think this? After

125

twenty-odd years? Maybe in Alena's fantasy he became some sort of a spirit, like a guardian angel.

For New Year's Eve Ben and Kiko and their friends departed by train to Kent where someone's parents kept a cottage. Neighbours from a street parallel to Gail's had dropped in an invitation to their party. She was glad.

On the night she found herself in a packed room. "This is Stuart." The hostess introduced her to a dwarfish man with a goatee. "Stuart is an outstanding anaesthetist." This Gail came instantly to believe, as merely standing next to him made her eyelids droop. She waited for the right moment, then excused herself and headed for the table bearing the drinks. Downing a large glass of red wine made a huge difference: now she could attach and detach herself at will. Soon a flamboyantly dressed woman with curly hair and a lively face approached her. Masha earned her living as a "life storyteller". On hearing Gail was a trainee therapist, she plunged into a tale about someone she knew, a man who after thirty years of happy marriage came home one night and on an impulse picked up a roasting skewer … now here was a fascinating slice of human psyche for Gail to get her teeth into. Conveniently, on the screen Big Ben struck midnight and a man in a purple sweater swung around and kissed Gail on the lips. Which was unexpected, but not entirely unwelcome. Easing herself into the New Year turned out to be not half as hard as she had feared. Now she could go home. While she groped in the dark bedroom for her jacket, a pair of arms pulled her into the profusion of coats. At first she took it to be the purple sweater extending his offer. But to her surprise her nose was pushed into a luxuriant mass of curls. They rolled around the dusty wool and winter furs, the air sour with semi-digested alcohol and naphthalene. First time Gail had engaged in something like this. Yet by the time she walked into her house the whole thing had gone from her head, like a story you overhear and instantly forget.

With the holiday still on, when the darkness started to seep in Gail would get in the car, as if off to visit someone, maybe Lyn who with her family occupied a floor of a palatial house in Blackheath and had always encouraged her to drop in. But invariably she would end up just navigating the streets. The wheel spinning smoothly in her hands, she caught other drivers' glances: strangers who trusted her with their lives. And this with no words spoken, just a nod here, the flick of an eyelid there, a naked wrist signal; those tacit gestures gave her courage. Each time she felt a surge of love swell in her like warm milk. It wasn't that she was hunting for someone but if something were to happen to lift her from her loneliness, she couldn't tell how and with whom, she wouldn't have refused, wouldn't have minded.

Today she parked in a narrow street in Greenwich where in the bygone era the two-up two-down terraces used to house the poor. These days a different tribe colonised them: city folks who migrated daily to the glass towers across the water. She leant against the iron railings and inhaled the river's smell.

As a child, on a summer holiday by a lake, she had seen a silver triangle leap up, spin in the air, plunge back with a great splash, then soar up again. With every leap more became visible: the glistening scales, the sharp fins. Then, as abruptly as it had been broken the stillness took over and there was only a white stain slowly floating away. What is it?, she asked Gillian. A fish, belly up, her sister said. To her horror, what Gail took to be a lavish performance was but a spasm of death.

Today, through the fog that swathed everything in gauze she made out a needle-like shape gliding over the flat water. The disembodied voices reached her surprisingly clear. "What did Mary say?" "What?" "Mary, what did she say when she heard?" "Oh. That she wasn't bothered." Evidently, whatever life had thrown at Mary, Mary had an effective way of dealing with it, unlike Gail. Then Gail heard footsteps—a man materialised from the mist and stood by the railings, not far from her: a thick short jacket, grey hair. She glanced around—except for the two of them the Thames Path was empty. One thing to fancy a chance encounter, but finding yourself with a stranger on an empty riverside quay was something else—the only way back was to pass him. The other way, after only a few yards, the path came to an abrupt end. But she refused to panic; she wasn't Alena with her crazy imaginings. As she stepped away from the railing the man briskly turned and vanished into the narrow passage at the end of which she had parked. She let a few minutes pass. Then she cautiously strolled forward. By the time she reached her car, there was no one there.

At home she poured herself a whisky from Eddie's bottle. Glass in hand, she trudged from room to room turning on all the lights—once more she was a girl alone in an empty house. A girl who used to devour her parents' collection of classics with the same speed her older sister worked through a catalogue of boyfriends. Emil, Emily, Charles, Charlotte, Gustav, Fyodor, Honoré, Leo—Gail was on first name terms with each of them, they were her dependable friends while she waited for someone to turn up whose touch would make her fully human.

The house ablaze around her, she camped on the sofa with the transistor radio for company; not having any ice cubes she switched to drinking the whisky out of the bottle. With the radio next to her ear, she listened to bursts of voices, eruptions of music. Out there the world was teeming with excitement and here she was scanning frequencies, twiddling the dial. On one station someone was telling them how in the middle of a service God had instructed him to learn a song in a different language each week. As there were over 6000 languages in the world the man said, he would be busy for years, the best thing he'd ever done. He sang a tune in Inuit and through the airwaves, the tang of his voice made blood rush to Gail's skin. If I were more musical, if I were better at languages I would do the same, she assured this unknown man. Sliding deeper into the sofa, the radio's metal edge digging into her cheek, she listened to some awe-inspiring organ music, the jingling of bells. Surprisingly, the ringing continued over the weather forecast. It rang through the house even when she took her ear off the set: there was someone at the door.

Her first thought was of Eddie. Ben was staying at Kiko's overnight and if he had forgotten his keys he would make more of a racket. At this hour she was expecting no one. It must be Eddie then. Eddie, bringing her his love. How could she have given up on him so easily? She patted smooth the cushions on the sofa, put the bottle away, and checked herself in the mirror: she was flushed and her left cheek showed the radio's ribbed imprint. But the shining honey fringe was still in place.

The man she opened the door to was older than Eddie and not as tall. He raised his finger as if doffing an imaginary hat and she noticed the grey mane, rock-'n'-roll style.

"Good evening. I apologise for disturbing, but we've met before."

She shielded her cheek with her hand, unable to remember ever meeting this man. Unless he was the same man she saw earlier by the river. She gripped the door ready to slam it in his face. "I'm sorry but I can't help you."

The man breathed out a cloud of white mist. "You're a psychotherapist aren't you? You told me so yourself."

The drink in her was evaporating fast and something else was flooding in, racing her pulse—fear. What was it that that doctor who had interviewed her, Dr. Erica Field, what was it she mentioned about a psychopath turning up on her doorstep? If Gail had listened to her advice and attended those psychiatric ward rounds, now she'd know what to look for. However, the man by the river wore a short jacket whereas this man was in a long heavy coat. But coats you can change.

"I'm sorry but I don't think we ever spoke."

"Don't you? We were on the train and I picked up your book. Something about objects." The man grinned an uneven sort of a smile and now she remembered the incident and that she had thought his legs were too short. "I've been thinking about having psychotherapy. And when I met you I thought, why not? Seeing you looked sympathetic. You take new patients?" He had a faint accent she couldn't place.

"I don't remember telling you where I live."

Sensing her apprehension the man kept a respectable distance. "I saw you coming in, I have a business in the area."

This was madness, she should shut the door at once. Surely, the man knew she wouldn't accept him for therapy just because they had once sat on the same train. And yet, this was oddly tempting. Suddenly she felt as though months had gone by without exchanging a word with anyone. At the back of her mind there was also the pressing issue of what to do if Alena Sokol chose not to return. And here was someone volunteering to fill her place.

"Sorry but I'm afraid this isn't how it works."

"How does it work then?" the man asked. "I've never done psychotherapy before." He had dark close-set eyes, his nose was arched, and his nostrils unusually elongated, like on ancient Assyrian or early Greek reliefs. Features that may appear exquisite but also menacing, depending on your frame of mind.

"You need to be recommended by someone," she said. "The person who does referrals."

"I see. Please, tell me then how can I contact this person?"

Having gone that far Gail was now not entirely averse to the prospect of going to look for Joanna Wilson's number. But to do this she would have to leave this man unattended at the open threshold of her house. What if he jumped in after her? As if he could hear her, the man's lips stretched into a loopy smile. "Just shut the door," he said. "I'm happy to wait outside."

130

TWENTY-TWO

To Gail's surprise Joanna Wilson phoned the next day. "Your man has called to make an appointment with me for an assessment," she said. "Not much fun being Serbian these days I suppose. Seems, Gail, you get all the foreigners. Where did you find him?"

"Word of mouth." Gail left it at that.

After Alex Avolos—the name the man wrote down for her—had left her she watched him from her "observation post" by the window walking up the road. It was too dark to see any details but in the passing headlights she saw his car: an old-fashioned Mercedes, black or midnight blue. The way he had sprung out of nowhere, the unexplained business he claimed to have in the area, it all sounded odd. On the other hand, should Joanna Wilson with her long practice deem him a suitable psychotherapy client, who was Gail to doubt her judgement? She would have no more reason not to see him than any Tom, Dick, or Harry who might, in hopefully the not too distant future, look her up in the Yellow Pages under Counselling and Psychotherapy.

A few days later Joanna called with her assessment. "An interesting character," she said. "A narcissist of the thick-skinned type but psychologically minded. An only child, had an over-close relationship with a controlling mother. Father disappeared when he was still young, so obviously there are issues to work through. Some time ago he had some sort of a stroke. Ever since suffers panic attacks, the reason he wants therapy. But the main issue about this fellow is that he lacks a paternal figure. That's why I've suggested he may prefer to see a male therapist."

"And his controlling mother, Joanna?" Gail objected. "What about his maternal figure!" Wasn't Joanna Wilson supposed to refer patients rather than snatch them away?

"Well in any case he isn't interested in a male therapist, he wants to see you. He seems rather intense; do you two know each other socially by any chance?"

"No, of course not!"

"Well, that's a relief. But I must warn you—this man's defences are *tremendously* strong. Bulletproof."

Her *Dictionary of Psychodynamic Psychotherapy* ran a comprehensive list of defence mechanisms: *repression, introjection, projective identification, splitting*, and so on—each a crutch to prop up a limping ego. The crutch a therapist has gradually to remove—rather a terrifying task—while keeping the person from fragmentation, otherwise falling on his nose.

She had arranged to see Alex Avolos on Tuesday, directly before Alena Sokol. Once you get your head into the psychoanalytic mode you'd better stay there, she presumed. Unlike with Alena she planned to charge this man a more realistic fee. That afternoon she had changed several times. After their impromptu encounter the other night she wanted to present herself as a professional, not a blowsy slob. Before the session she removed from the wall Eddie's seaside painting. The small hole from the nail oozed a tear of fine dust, which she quickly swept up.

When Alex Avolos arrived he removed his coat, hung it on the hook on the door and politely stood in the middle of the room. She immediately recognised the wristwatch with its old-fashioned fluorescent dial. In his white shirt, unbuttoned at the neck, and sharply creased trousers Alex Avolos looked like one of those types in Italian films: men who populate darkened bars, nonchalantly checking themselves in the chrome of the espresso machine before emerging into the sun-bleached street to take on the opposite sex. But then she remembered that this man actually came from where a war was in full swing.

"Shall I pay you now?" He reached in his back pocket. "How much?"

"Not now. I'll give you an invoice at the end of the month." She asked him to write down his name and address and as he placed the paper on her desk she noticed in the metal shade of the lamp that, curiously, his name read Solova back to front. She had to look twice but here it was, as if fate was at work: Avolos—Solova—Sokolova.

She gestured to the chair. "Please sit down."

Alex Avolos glanced at the couch. "You don't want me to lie down and free associate?"

"The couch's not in use, not for the time being."

His lips twitched. His cheeks had the bluish tint dark men acquire a few hours after they have shaved. "So when will the time being come into being? Providing the future is indeterminate or even merely potential."

Not quite catching what he meant Gail refrained from saying anything. Once they were both seated Alex Avolos caressed the leather armrests. "Hmm ... Top grain, full aniline. Not cheap." It was not only the Swiss watch on his wrist that reminded her of her father, there were also his hands, slim and covered with dark hairs, on his fingers too. Monkey's hands she used to call them.

With the same thoroughness with which he had inspected the room the man now studied the length of her, each detail. To hide how self-conscious she felt Gail tightened her neck and stomach. How was she to speak to this man old enough to be her father?

"First I want you to know that everything you will tell me is confidential. We could start by—"

Alex Avolos lifted himself from the chair and readjusted its carefully chosen angle to face her squarely. "Whoever sat here before didn't want to look at you. Their loss, I say."

Now she saw what made his smile skewed: a slash cut across his upper lip, a short thin scar: from a childhood accident, she imagined. In the kitchen on the floor below, Ben could be heard chatting on the phone. Gail was grateful he had agreed to stay. At least today, her first time with this stranger.

"Your son?" The man pointed to the floor. She made a neutral movement with her head. Accepting her terms, he nodded. "I understand. In my business people also tell me confidential things, you'd be surprised."

"What business is this?"

"Dry cleaning. I have dry cleaning shops all over the place: Blackheath, Dulwich, Stockwell. Can't you smell it on me?"

Instinctively Gail sucked in air through her nose. "No."

"It's the perc. Perchloroethylene. Men can't smell it but women can." She suppressed her irritation; this man, first he provokes her into making a fool of herself, and then he calls her a lesser woman. "Dry cleaning wasn't always my business; I did other things, all sorts," the man explained, looking straight at her. "But these days, I have a problem to think of even one thing to get me out of bed."

"And what might this one thing be?" She hoped this didn't sound like a prompt to reveal something intimate.

"Today it was coming to you. And it worked! And you, what do you wish for when you wake up?"

The moment when a patient asks a personal question, a question that in normal circumstances you might be willing to answer. But as a therapist, that's not what you do. Because, ultimately, how would Alex Avolos benefit from knowing that